Anonymous

Macalpine

Or, on Scottish Ground. A novel. Part 1

Anonymous

Macalpine
Or, on Scottish Ground. A novel. Part 1

ISBN/EAN: 9783337051617

Printed in Europe, USA, Canada, Australia, Japan

Cover: Foto ©Andreas Hilbeck / pixelio.de

More available books at **www.hansebooks.com**

MACALPINE;

OR,

ON SCOTTISH GROUND.

A Novel.

●

"Who aspires
To genuine greatness
Temper with the sternness of the brain
Thoughts motherly and meek as woman█
Books, leisure, perfect freedom, and the█
Man holds with week-day man:
These are the do█
By which true sway doth mount."
—WORD█

●

VOL. I.

●

LONDON:
SAMPSON LOW, MARSTON, LOW, & SEARLE,
CROWN BUILDINGS, 188 FLEET STREET.
1872.

MACALPINE;

OR,

ON SCOTTISH GROUND.

CHAPTER I.

'HE estate of Morven, in the Grampians, com-
ences on the west with the village of that
ame, lying at the foot of a conically-shaped
ill, thickly grown with the fir-tree. Through
ie village northwards, in a semicircle, making
)r high ground at the west side of the hill,
ins the turnpike road, which overlooks the
ipid river—refreshing to eye and ear as it
ins its pebbly course amid the stately firs and
ines that clothe the high and steep banks, and
;retch their shaded and dense magnificence
pon the brows of the mountains. Immedi-
tely at the back of this hill stands another of

VOL. I.   A

similar shape and size. Twin hills, they present
to each other rocky and almost perpendicular
sides. At the foot a roadway had been con-
structed, but, narrow and liable to be blocked
up by pieces of fallen rock, it fell into disuse by
travellers, who had at one time attempted to
make of it a short cut off the turnpike road.
The sight of a deserted road often arouses the
fancy no less than a decayed and deserted
mansion, and in each case some legend has
frequently to account for the ruin. Although
physical imperfections sufficiently accounted for
the desertion of the "pass" roadway, super-
stition had handed down, about its immediate
region, more than one tale of mysterious
appearances of denizens of other spheres than
the plain and homely earth, and of mysterious
disappearances of mortals who had held
communion with them. The estate of Morven
belonged to the Chief of the Macalpines,—the
oldest in descent, and at one time the greatest
and proudest of the lairds of the county.

The common belief was, that some hag or witch had cast a blight upon the road and upon those who made it, for having by its cutting dispossessed her of a hut at the mouth of the pass, in which she had delighted to spend her splenetic life. The fortunes of the laird, to continue the idle report, had visibly declined since the day the hag had prophesied their fall ; and although upon the road ceasing to be used, the hag was specially privileged to veer down upon her old site, and thereupon ventured upon revealing some after-luck for the fallen lairds of Morven, still the blight was on the family as well as on the road; and the men and women who congregated in the village and the cottages and by the hill-sides, thought of the hag of Morven Pass when they heard of each new blow to the tottering house of Macalpine.

Towards the east of this passage or pass it gradually widens, ending a few yards from a stream which runs beyond the entrance in a

dell, where are, or were, trees of several
varieties, dense and luxuriant in spring and
summer from the nurture of the flowing water.
Over this hollow, at the time of the opening of
the tale, was a long narrow wooden bridge,
scarcely, perhaps, entitled to the dignity of
that name, since it consisted of but three
planks upheld by stakes driven into the banks
of the stream, with some rude iron fastenings
at the middle.   It admitted only of one
pedestrian crossing at a time, and was sufficiently dangerous to excite apprehension for
the safety of any irate contenders for preced-
ence who might quarrel towards its centre, as
two rival chiefs at enmity were said once on a
time to have done.   But the spot was far
from calculated to engender thoughts of strife
or rivalry.   The bosky dell was one of sweet
and romantic loveliness, such as the imagination, fatigued by the sublimity of the high
regions without, might take refuge in, and the
fancy tickle itself with—

"Such sights as youthful poets dream,
On summer's eve by haunted stream."

The stream had met in one respect the same
fate as the road—it was haunted. The super-
stitious, the young and the playful, dwelling
in the regions of Morven, oft lingered at the
Falloch Bridge in the hope that some inhabi-
tant of the dark water beneath would rise and
reveal their fortune, or that of some departed
friend.

Here, ere the decline of a summer night, Alan
Macalpine found himself after a long day's
excursion. He lay down for a few minutes
before he passed upon the bridge, his gaze
resting on the smooth-flowing stream. The
soothing influence of the placid water close upon
the nightfall, when all nature indicates coming repose, as the general stillness is broken by
the ripple of the wave upon some jutting bank,
was felt by the traveller, and enjoyed after the
active pleasures of the day. Now, as often
before, he dwelt in fanciful regions, peopling

the river-bed with strange creations, and with
dreamy longing throwing himself into hope
that his fanciful visions might realise themselves in actual appearances, to tell him of the
world beyond. It was the fancy of the poet,
not the material longing of the worldling.
Alan had no future of anxious fortune before
him ; he was content enough. And he rose as
usual, and went his way after his musing,
knowing that imagination made the world.

Where he had lain, the bridge was partly
concealed by the branches of an overhanging
tree, and Alan was already partly across ere
his longing fancy seemed to have met with a
response. Half-way across the bridge a fairy-
like form was looking into the water gliding
beneath, as unawares as the stream itself of his
approach. Alan's first impulse was not to dis-
turb what his fancy was inclined to accept as
the spirit of the stream. To that neighbourhood, in the time of this history, though 'tis
not full forty years since, fashion never trans-

ported itself. The peasant girls' attire seldom
went further than the plain coarseness which
supplied simple natural requirements. Here,
stood, however, to his active fancy what seemed
the airy form of a nymph, lulled by the voices
in the watery bed on which she gazed.

> " And she was fair ! oh, fairer floated never
> The foam-born goddess fresh from ocean's stream.
> Hers was perchance the mystic form that ever
> Had haunted with delight my boyhood's dream."

Courage was not wanting in Alan. He possessed in large share the manliness of a simple
heart ; yet, modest in the extreme, it was only
the unreality present to his imagination which
gave him the spur to an adventure. Just as
the fair vision slightly stirred, indicating her
humanity by the movement of the frail material on which she stood, he whispered an
address to her, dictated by the thought with
which she had seemed to him to be rapt :

> " Oh, the running of the river,
> And the silence of the stars."

She started, and confusedly ran forward *
rather than back, as if to make her way past
on the narrow bridge.

"Now you clearly show," said Alan, "you are
no fairy, or you would not require the bridge.
Both of us being mortals, either you or I must
get back;" so saying, he drew quickly back, and
the lady tripped, too confused to answer, forward upon the bank. There, however, recalling
her thoughts from their wanderings "in fairy-
land forlorn," she regarded Alan with an animated expression, from which all sense of the
awkwardness of the encounter had vanished.
She had obtained a full sense of security in the
open and gentlemanly bearing of her companion, and the combination of strength and
manly honest openness which his appearance bore. He was about six feet in height,
rather slender than massive, dark in complexion, pale rather than ruddy ; the melancholy which might be seen in his features was
not sadness, but sensibility and thought, yet

not even that was too pronounced to call attention from the frankness and ease of his
bearing.

"I am sorry to be so little of the fairy, that
I must put you to the risk of again using the
bridge," the lady said. There was no tone of
archness in her voice, but it struck Alan that
the speaker, perhaps unconsciously, possessed
the quality. If it were so, tenderness spoke in
her countenance. The fair luxuriance of complexion, the lithe ease of the graceful figure,
were forgot in the charm of the face, expressive
of delicate and true love.

" My love of the marvellous can be satisfied
with less cost than your disappearance in the
stream. I am content to find contemplating
the legendary water one whom I might ima-
gine its presiding spirit," he answered.

"The illusion is dispelled," she said, without
a blush. The tone of the speaker had contained no accent either of flattery or mock ; and
the lady felt only the romantic fervour of her

companion, while she herself had been inclined
to smile.

"I am so often displeased with realities,"
said the other, now himself smiling, "that I
do not care to part with happy illusions
readily."

"I fear that my neighbourhood would not
supply the illusion you relish," she observed
with half-suppressed gaiety ; and she turned
as if to bid Alan a "good-night." He was in
no mood to be parted with so readily. He
expressed the surprise he had received in the
encounter. A lady and a stranger alone at
such a place and at such an hour !—Had she
lost her way, or been separated from a party of
travellers ? It was not so. She was near her
own home. Alan expressed his surprise to hear
it. "My fathers before me," said he, "have
for centuries called a circuit of many miles
round this neighbourhood their own ; and I
have for years known every man and woman
in it." Alan spoke in a tone of sadness which

he could not conceal. The lady was struck by
his altered tone, and looked again, instinctively,
as if searching for an explanation in the face
of the speaker of the subdued melancholy
in his voice.

"You are then" —— hesitating with the
name of the laird.

"A Macalpine," he said. "Once upon a time
no one could have been in Morven for an hour
without knowing that name; now our lands
go to a stranger—and we become forgotten."
He spoke with a bitterness rare to him. His
companion felt the misfortune of her remark.
But she really had heard of the Macalpines
that very day; and she at once, with an eager
happiness which pleased the young Highlander,
corrected the mistake.

"It seems like a maudlin grief to speak in
this way; but for many days I have scarcely
spoken to a human being except my father;
and now that fate has given me the ear of one
whom my fancy might have thought an in-

habitant of another world, I would seem to wish to pour out my selfish woes without ceasing."

"Proceed with your story ; it cannot be all melancholy. Remember I have none," said his companion, moved.

"Then you are truly evolved from the water," cried Alan, returning to pleasantry.

She was returning to Finzean, the farm of Oliver Arnot, her uncle, a tenant on the property which had belonged to the Macalpines, and a friend of Alan himself.

Fair woman had been hitherto in Alan Macalpine's life only a distant dream. The dream to-night he in his jubilance thought was realising itself. He felt transported by the charms of female loveliness into a new region. The past with him had been hard and dry, irrespective of his indulgence of his fancy, and the practice of an active kindly spirit towards his fellows. He had been happy : amid all the melancholy of his situation and of his earnest spirit, his

days, if not days of mirth and pleasure, gave
him happiness ; nature and his daily work had
many charms for him. Yet there was a void.
No heart of woman—nor of man—had in his
career united its deeper emotions with his own.
He was solitary. Now he felt lured away by
the spontaneity of his whole being ; a new
experience of a glory and a freshness of the
dream :—

> " A dreamer strayed,
> And there I saw her ! a sweet welcome wonder
> Through all my sense her floating image sent,
> From those fair brows of hers and sweet eyes under ;
> And something in me drew me where she went."

Alan and Ellen Lee emerged from the wood,
which terminated at the opening into the pass,
and walked over the purple-clad ground which
stretched beyond. It was as if the barrier of
previous ignorance of each other had not
existed. In the presence of a calm which is
eternal, though there be storms which come
and go upon the surface—in the living summer,
treading upon the flowery vigorous wild of

nature, they forgot that they had met for the
first time. The Highlander felt, in viewing
the grandeur and beauty of the place, a new
wonder—that the feeling was shared by a companion at once susceptible and tenacious like
himself of impressions of the beautiful. A
new enthusiasm had arisen in the heart of
each, which neither cared to check, so natural
and delicious was it. To approach the place of
parting was to both a positive pain. They had
already rendered to each other, impersonal as
was most of their speech, a devotion silent but
unrestrained.

The fragrance of the flower may not be
wasted in the desert air, though the traveller
see it not ; nor may be lost the sweetness of
woman, though she pass away beyond where is
felt the secret of her power.

CHAPTER II.

ADVERSITY often gives a pungency to existence, to make it more relished than had an even prosperity bound it. Alan Macalpine had never known else than the scant treasury which had been the lot of the later generations of his family, who had been ruined by their litigious and also carelessly generous spirits. The last strokes of evil fortune had come in Alan's own day. He found even such smiles as brightened his earlier years, later on turned into darkness. As his father, Roderick, fell into hopeless bankruptcy, society avoided him; and Alan, an only child, strayed after his own way, to find in the pleasures of a country life, and in communion with the nature around and with self, more than recompense for the life which prosperity would have brought him. But the son of Roderick Macalpine, now in his twenty-fourth year, had grown in the knowledge that there are other wants to be satisfied than those procurable through rod or gun, or the mysterious beauties of earth and air. Never had he surrendered his faith in the future, though the demon of utter decay often seemed about to crush his house. The powerful frame of Roderick Macalpine had swung to and fro with hasty stride, and his dark eyes had sat fiercely in his head, as if in defiance of the powers of fate which had so long belaboured him, as he passed through the village of Morven on that day when he bade a final adieu to Morven Castle, to take up his abode in a small lodge near by; and his first moments in his new and humble residence had been used in writing to his solicitor pages of abuse of judges, laws, and lawyers, with instructions for a new appeal to the courts of law. The son, bracing himself to a reconciliation with fate, more than retained his former faith.

Alan did not follow a profession, nor had he intended to follow one. He had attended college in Edinburgh, and taken a degree; that satisfied him that he had capacity for mental labour; and now, in the first moments of his fallen fortunes, he prepared himself to embrace the study of the law. His father deemed service in a writer's office the first step; but the result of this design was a harsh experience, which embittered Alan's sensitive heart. The solitary youth came of a race which had heaped its gold in the lap of the law; but now its dispensers had nothing more to seek of the impoverished Macalpines. Alan found himself of no account as the son of a ruined laird among the legal scribes of the Scottish metropolis, and there were none who had for him else than the glib civility of the heartless man of the world. He retired with disgust, determined, in the ardour of his young heart, that subsistence and something more should be found where his heart was fixed—on the congenial soil of his native county. He set to work with right good-will at learning the ordinary branches of agricultural business ; and his limited previous knowledge, casually acquired, in course of a few years developed into rare skill and aptitude in the breeding and treatment of cattle. Thus it was that at twenty-four he was a stock-farmer, and an occasional instructor of villagers and young men and women of the mountain-side. Young Macalpine required for himself an extremely moderate share of the world's gear. He was poor and content : it is the rich who are devoured with the passion to become richer, falsely imagining that the poor are ever in envy of their fortune. Alan kept away from the side of Mammon, which he might have courted with a wild fury, for the demon passions of his fathers were in him, yet subdued. Occasionally in the lone nights, when the fancy rouses strong at some touch of the external world, there rushed up into his throat and upon his brain the red-hot blood of ambition to reconquer the old land by the might of the new world's enterprise. But he was not passion's slave ; preferring, not out of indolence but reason, freedom of soul and the unembarrassed sweets of a simple existence ; and he nourished no vain desires after his restoration to Morven, much as his fancy had at times loved to dream of the possibility.

CHAPTER III.

ELLEN LEE was the niece of an extensive stockowner of the county, who was married, but had no family of his own. In a more than pliant hour, the jovial Oliver Arnot, her maternal uncle, found himself the lord of whatever charms the irrepressible Jess Scoular could boast. This widow had enjoyed the delicious gratification of power over one victim of her conjugal tie only long enough to desire its continuance over another. Her restless spirit had no sooner reasserted itself, after a short period of mourning, than it was engaged in attacking the easy defences which rounded the core of Oliver Arnot of Finzean. Her son and only child, the long-legged and "ill-faured" Tam, went with her to Finzean, where he lived—years developing the ungainly strength of the youth

—until he became troublesome to his stepfather,
and was sent to another farm in the county,
where the energy of his blood hardly found a
taming in the driving of the wildest cattle, and
exercises after the flocks upon the steepest hills.
Had Finzean been cleared also of its mistress,
the peace of its master would have been complete, though his purse was unquestionably the
weightier by her management. The softer side
of the stockowner had need of some nourishment, and that it had not received. His
marriage was a grief to him, of which, however,
there were no outward signs. Were a favourite
bull ill, Jess Arnot was the woman to bring it
round. In her powerful wild-looking eye there
dwelt some fascination for the lower animals.
On them she appeared to cast a species of
affection too rough for frail humanity; and
the cow seemed bound to rejoice with a new
vigour under the caressing ministrations of
the woman. She had no music in her soul, and
her husband was fond of song; nay, played

jigs and reels himself upon the fiddle, to which
Jess was known to dance at the Auld Yules
with Wat McTavish, the schoolmaster and re-
puted poacher ;—dancing with a fling, swing,
and kick, even without the influence of the
strong waters of the Highlands, which would
have staggered the modern war-dancers, and
given a permanent shock to the nervous sys-
tems of the languid walkers of the fashionable
ball-room. The void in the heart of the good-
humoured farmer, which Mrs Arnot did not
supply, was at last filled by a sister of his own,
a widow, dying and leaving to his charge her
only child, Ellen.

Arnot's sister and he had been estranged
ever after she had left her father's house, in
consequence of some passages in her life which
seem to have shocked the rigid society in
which she lived. Possibly, through this
estrangement, deeply regretted by the farmer,
her daughter may have been all the more
welcome. Upon her life, which had already

known twenty-two summers when she came
to Finzean, shadows had been cast without
impairing the vitality of her happy temper.
The new scene to which she came awakened
suddenly a sense as of delicious roving in a
new world ; it was the partial realisation of
many a dream in a life in which a yearning
for romance and a distant sense of its dangers
were strangely mixed.

CHAPTER IV.

THE house of Finzean lay not far off from the Falloch Bridge, though Alan Macalpine and his companion made the distance an hour's walk. It was a structure of some pretension, and had once been the dwelling of a laird whose property had been taken in at considerable cost by the grandfather of Roderick Macalpine. A low whitewashed building, upon which architecture had expended no ingenuity, its consideration lay in a great range of breadth, and a size of window not common in old country mansions. Oliver Arnot was by his dwelling, as much as by his large possession of cattle and sheep, a man looked up to by his kith and kin of the country round. His wife was proud of her lord's position in this respect, and demanded its recognition on every available opportunity. The quiet worthy farmer himself was shamed by many of the demonstrations of his spouse; so much so, that it often became a wonder to himself, as to others, how or by what means he became the husband of, in many respects, so ill-assorted a partner as Jess Scoular. Mrs Arnot had a particular fancy for her once great neighbour, Roderick Macalpine. Hers was one of those natures, like his own, in which deliberate reflection plays little part. To fine instincts they were accessible, as to the worst, but there was no guarantee whatever that they would be in the right. Abstractions, either of justice or truth, were unknown to them, and had they been so, would have been scorned by their quick and swelling tempers. While she bespattered the name of Roderick Macalpine with her admiration, she sometimes shook her head at that of his son. The life she admired was grand and glowing.

"The laird's een," she would say, "could dazzle an eagle's, and his voice be heard here,

cryin' on Ben Lomond.   As for the learnin', gin
ye can show me what the son 's made o't, I 'll believe then, gude master.   Na, na, speak na ill o'
the laird ; he 's a braw man.   The schoolhouse 'll
no bring siller to buy back the auld lands."

The niece of Mrs Arnot had no sooner
entered the gateway at Finzean than she was
accosted by that lady with an inquiry into the
cause of her prolonged absence.

"Odd, Ellen, lass, I thocht ye were awa
wi' the kelpies.   Far hae ye been wanderin'
at this time o' nicht ?—and ye hae a man
too ! "—as Alan came behind.   " Mercy, lass !
ye 'r an unco gipsy.   Oh, it 's you, Mister
Alan ! I hadna thocht ye kent my niece.   But
ye 'r welcome—the son o' the Laird o' Morven
is ever welcome here, and to a' its belongings.
Thae were sad days for Morven when the laird
gaed doun the dyke and ower the water.
But ye 'll get to the Indies yet, an' win back
the lands."   As her tongue thus ran on, without opportunity given for reply, Ellen and Alan

were ushered into her dwelling, whose interior revealed more comfort and refinement than would have been believed, judging from the rough address of its mistress. Moving forward with energetic rather than hasty strides, her progress was impeded first by several dogs, ever desirous to procure the notice of their mistress; and again, as she entered the sitting-room, by her son Tam, who, lazily skulking in the doorway, allowed his mother, in the dark, to come unawares upon his ungainly form, and fall heavily over him. "Tam, ye deil," she cried out, as she picked herself up, "ye 'll ne'er gae far ye 'r wanted, but are aye i' the road like an ill hack-log."

Upon hearing something was wrong, the dogs barked, the women servants ran about, and the house was at once in a scene of great commotion when it became known that harm had come to the female in the collision.

"Odds, Mrs Arnot," said the master, "it 's not like you to be sae soft."

"Ay, there it is, gudeman; ye'll send me murder-haste after a puir cow, but gin I'm hurt, I can bide sae."

"Na, na, wife; we'll ha' ye bandaged; and here is my good friend Mr Alan, something of a doctor I ken, will do the work," said the farmer, his face reddening with suppressed laughter—his sense of the ridiculous in the encounter getting the better of his concern for his spouse. To her harsh features a blackish eye was now to be added, but this sturdy member of her sex refused to be comforted with poultice or bandage, and sat blinking at guests and household.

In this way, amid a strange mingling of romance and humour, did Alan Macalpine make the acquaintance of Ellen Lee. In communion with the lively spirit of Ellen, Alan's thoughts were borne clear off the rough days through which he had recently passed. Ellen too learned to forget for a time past cares, and the harsh character of her female companion;

in the growth of her love the shadows of her
early years became as the dark morning clouds
floating away before the brightness of the coming noon. It seemed to her the realisation of a
hope.

That there was any disparity in their relative
circumstances to justify them in holding aloof
from each other, ere they stepped into that
magic circle from which there is no wrenching
except to the danger of both or one, neither
saw. There was an affinity from the first, and
other considerations there were none, except
that Alan's prudence recognised that his
material provision for the future required to
be looked in the face. The proud spirit of his
father had always rebelled against Alan's buy-
ing and selling cattle, and instructing peasants
in the rudiments of knowledge, but his re-
bellion was suppressed before the calm reason-
ing intellect of the son. Had he known, however, that that son had further compromised the
dignity of the Macalpines by consorting with

the niece of one of his former tenants, curses loud and deep would have fallen. But he was too self-engrossed to perceive the evil knot, to him, that was being tied. There was one person, however, whose keen eyesight would have detected the nature of the intimacy between the pair, though it had been made a secret, which it was not in any respect. This was Mrs Arnot. She tried to believe that it was only idle humour on the part of both, which must end in separation, until months passed away and there was no cessation of companionship. The mother of Mr Thomas Scoular had desired, with every fibre of her rough heart, to see her son united to the niece of her husband and heiress of his wealth. What could she do to stop the progress of this scheme-marring affection? She possessed no elixir to drive away love from the human breast, as she did the diseases of the cow and horse. She had no power of lock and key, or she might have tried physical force, of which she was more a mistress than of the soft persuasions of life. The loud language with which now and then she indicated her disapprobation of her niece's conduct, was received as the fresh-spirited youth, stepping into the sunny lawn, hears the howl of the kennelled cur which barks at the step, as it is its nature to do. Alan and Ellen continued the conjunction of their spirits. A week and more would pass, during which he was off in distant parts of the country, and a few days would pass when he was at home without seeing Ellen, still they contrived never to be long absent from each other. At Finzean she was busy in learning the details of the female branches of farm-work, her instruction being occasionally assisted also there by Alan himself, who broke in upon the learned demonstrations of her uncle or his wife. He would laugh over the awkwardness of her first efforts to milk a cow or make butter. Some might have expected to find from her appearance a fine-ladyism which would set her above engaging in such occupations; but her

activity refused no occupation which conduced
to her usefulness or health of body or of mind.
Alan taught her to ride, to climb hills, and to
row on the loch.   A favourite occupation was
in attending to the flowers in her uncle's garden, partly perhaps because it reminded her of
the home which was gone for ever from her.
To the sublime mountains her tender gaze had
at the first turned only with awe ; they were
new to her, and beyond the springs of her old
delight.   It was only in the company of Alan
that she learned to blend their high aspect in
her imagination with all that was heroic and
grand.   The soft features of her being were
still present, though the pictures conjured up
to her of brave men who had fallen there, and
whose restless spirits were supposed to hover
in the storms with which their own bold
natures had held communion, stirred the
depths of her blood.   She was a new woman
in these few months ; bolder, more spirited in
her mental purposes as in her bodily action ;

while she was still the tender lover of all calling for attachment.

In her conversations with Alan self formed generally small part, in contradiction to the common case of those so situated. Ellen, at times, thought she would have preferred to rest more upon their own histories, doings, and hopes. The abstractions of life, embodied even in the deepest poetry of humanity, are not so attractive to the feminine as to the male heart; Alan was much given to musing and dilating on these. Occasionally Ellen would ask herself whether this were not a dream, in which Alan played the part of an insubstantial spirit of the mountain, rather than of a real flesh and blood lover. Did this arise, she asked herself, from the difference in their rank? It was not from want of display of his affection for her; perhaps it was because he had not spoken of marriage. With men accustomed to find pleasure in the exercise of intellect and heart, woman is not the consummation of all things, even when that one woman approaches who is to journey on with them through their days: woman's hand in such a case reaches already to the hour upon the dial which is to mark their absorption in another life.

CHAPTER V.

ONE morning in autumn it was observed, by the whole household in Finzean, that the usually healthy appetite of Mr Oliver Arnot was not in strength. The porridge dish was only half empty. Two eggs more than usual remained for the domestics : the coffee was indeed all drunk, but the toast-rack contained two or three slices which were not usually found there at the conclusion of the morning repast. It was known in the kitchen that the defaulter was the master ; for the mistress, though possessing a keen appetite for many things, was not inordinately disposed to quantities of viands. Oliver Arnot's appetite this morning was mastered by the qualms of anxiety. He felt ill and depressed, and disposed positively to be out of temper. He drew up his portly

form before the mirror, he walked in his garden and cut twigs off a tree, all to convince
himself that he ought to be calm. Now, the
occasion of all this was, that he was struck to
the quick with the thought that the niece
who was left to his honest care was in danger.
He had long shut his conscience to the urgings
of his wife, as he did his ears to most of her
grievances. But time had brought conviction,
and the feeling had also grown upon him that
something should be done. With a man of his
temperament anything out of the way was
unpleasant. He grew feverish and disposed to
go in for any work, however disagreeable, in
the hope that it would divert his thoughts.
As he sat at breakfast this morning, his manner
to his niece was short and constrained, and
Ellen felt that a scene was impending in
which she was to form an actor.

That it concerned her intimacy with Alan
Macalpine, she had no doubt. He could not
conceal his thoughts when Ellen came into

the room : his eyes rested upon a small portrait of young Macalpine that hung upon the wall, and he started like a guilty thing as she came quietly in while he was so occupied. Was it then a dream after all, from which impended a rude awaking—this period during which the days had coursed on in uninterrupted joy, a green spot on which she stood but for a moment, on her journey to a blank unknown region of desert land? She felt bitterly the curse which the conventionalities of the world frames for itself, to destroy the peace of its people. "Ellen, you 're wanted by your uncle," Mrs Arnot had said, in calm measured tone, which was meant for a kindly contrast with the severity of the encounter thereby indicated as to be undergone elsewhere ; but which did not conceal from Ellen the delight in her pain.

Oliver Arnot was seated in the best room of the house, used but once a year when the Auld Yule feast was on. The furniture was antiquated and undusted; the air was old and depressing. He occupied its highest chair, chokeful rather of uneasiness than dignity, though feeling the necessity of appeasing the requirements of his position by a formality which it was his nature to detest.

"Take a seat, Ellen," were his words when she entered, wearing on her countenance that easy weight of martyrdom naturally assumed by a pretty woman when called to account for the venial offence of permitting her attractions to assert their unwary power.

She sat with a coolness which somewhat disarmed her uncle. She knew she was poor and without a home, and felt what, by her uncle's displeasure, she might forfeit. Beyond all, she thought how his displeasure would cut her off from an intercourse which had been rich to her in joy. Yet, as fate determined, she would be prepared.

"Ellen, this will not do;" and Arnot turned himself in his chair and stopped—a speech which the intended moralist had prepared having vanished from his memory.

Ellen waited with patience that her monitor should unfold himself; but he failed to get under weigh, and she felt sorry for his confusion, though she could not well come to the rescue.

She now imagined that her days at Finzean had ended. In one moment she knew her course. She must go forth upon the open world and earn her bread, struggling with the dense and eager crowds.

For this emergency a moment's resolution prepared her; a moment of pain which was not anguish, because she felt equal to the demands that were to be cast upon her.

After various movements, the farmer remembered something of the first considerations of the case; his pointed argument was gone.

"I'll tell you, Ellen, things are changed; it's not as in my young days when a young man'd take to a young woman, and they had

no heed o' father or mither sae lang as a bow o'
meal was to be got for little, and broth wi' a
bit mutton sooming i' tap i' pot, like a moose,
served a family for a week.   I'm no thinking
they're better noo than they were.   There's
Wat McTavish, the schoolmaster, married to
the huzzie Barbara Inglis, frae the south, wi'
her fine notions o' gentility, and her father only
a puir horse-doctor,—I'm thinking puir Wat's
poaching comes at times o' her taste for finery.
'Na, na,' said her father, when Wat was after
her; but Wat the chield sent Inglis some
braces o' grouse and muirfowl and hares, and I
hae it that Wat passed for a sma' laird amang
them, whiles he was but a spankin dominie;
and he brings hame the lassie wi a tocher o' a
hunder pounds, and a bit extravagant notions
which set Wat's brains aboot, and into the
claws o' the law, I'm thinking,—puir Wat;
and a' for love o' a handsome cummer wi' a
weel-clad back and bonnie flowers on her head,
come o' her gentility what likes ; things are no

what they were, dinna ye see that? we maun mind the new roads." He came to a pause, feeling that his argument, as he saw it, was exhausted by the illustration of Wat McTavish's case.

Ellen felt for the time a mastery over the good-natured man. "I am not old enough to have observed the old state of things so as to compare with the present, but my mother has often told me it was more natural the life in former days."

"Ay, ay, that's it, natural it was, and it's not so now," he cried, breathlessly, thinking that he might be assisted good naturedly to the climax which he desired so much to reach by a round and safe path. "There's a vast difference in the feelings o' men, Ellen; there's nae such thing i' this time as love. I'll no accuse others, and spare mysel'. No. Dae ye think Mistress Scoular married your uncle for love? no that I would say that to her, and ye'r discreet, an'll no repeat this, for truth's

often ugly and needs the breeks. Na, na,
Mistress Scoular, though she'll be mistress
here sae lang as God spares her, worthy and
valuable woman—though her spirits be high at
a time—married me not for love;" and here,
drawn into a confession more painful than he
had believed it would have been, he drew his
hand over his face and hid a grief which stood
in his eye. Perhaps it was that the ghost of
an old love had risen within him, when he had
believed as did the young heart before him
which he desired to chill. "O Ellen, Ellen!"
he resumed, "ye'll be deceived if ye think
there's only love to count upon between man
and woman."

"Affection has not died out of the world,"
she said, with a low voice, not knowing exactly
how to meet these distant sallies, but affected
at her uncle's emotion.

"It's the heart that's noo ta'en up wi' the
world's gear—it's chocked up and poisoned
like a dead well and only foulness pours in it.

There's nae sense in't a bit; but it's the
fashion, and we maun conform. It's the
core that's wrang—nae doot o' that ; it's never
been livin' i' the new times, a' rotten wi' vanities. In my young days youth was youth,
and nae blythe maid but had her sweethearts
wha'd break their necks, forbye their hearts,
after her; and as for lovin' anything else,
they'd hae blown their brains out first. A'
for love, was the motto o' that time. Doun in
my father's barn I hae seen a dozen couples
tripping it without a guinea-piece i' the pouch
o' ane of them, and yet they made the world
the richer and the happier by the next Auld
Yule ; and there were them wi' twa thousand
sheep and twenty heed o' black cattle would be
after ane o' the lasses, and been left standing
for a lad wi' neither pedigree nor bawbees, but
just his lithe step and his bright een and his
merry fancy. See na ye that noo? Besides,
lass," he continued, after a pause which Ellen
did not break ; " I'm thinkin' it's no in accord-

ance wi' your duty to be gaein' on as ye do wi'
Mr Alan Macalpine."

"My duty to whom, uncle?" asked Ellen,
now somewhat hurt.

"To everybody concerned, lassie," said he,
in his heart puzzled to answer definitely.

" I can see no sin," she said, boldly, "in doing
what the whole world has ever done from
the day that God gave Eve to Adam as a companion and helpmate."

"That's it just; did Providence intend you
for this young man?"   Finding himself, he
knew not where in the argument, Oliver Arnot
preferred casting its burthen upon Ellen.

"I know not, for revelations are not made
now as of old times.   In the absence of this
revelation therefore, uncle, we may be content
to believe in what is not wrong in itself; if Mr
Macalpine chooses my company and I give it,
we need look for no other approval—than
yours, uncle, which I thought I had."

There was a confidence in her tone which

nettled while it surprised Arnot. Was this his
tender, laughing niece! Stronger natures, or
conventionally higher, calling "these delicate
creatures ours," fancy such always yielding
like a dying strain. But let these ruder be-
ware. The delicate ones are struck to no uncertain sound.

"My sister's only child will no do wrang in
the eyes o' the world without knowing o 't.
You 're young, lassie, to speak so proudly.
Where got ye that tongue? You 're ower fast.
If it be not your duty to some, what say you to
me alone? Am I not your nearest bluid, and
would be your true friend to the end o' the
chapter, ay and after; and hae I no right to
say my mind upon ye if things gae wrang. It 's
no doin' your duty to me, Ellen Lee, that the
haill country side sees ye dancing aboot wi' the
son o' the auld laird; a' speak o 't, and your
weel thrashed wi' their clashing tongues, no
that I mind that muckle; it 's wrang whether
the country side sees it or no; though ye were

together in the dark only, that's no what
should be. Ellen Lee can never be, should
never be, the wife of Alan Macalpine, even if
that be what the young man means."

Ellen started to her feet, aroused with indignation.

It choked her with anguish that her mother's
brother seemed to tread upon his sister's dark
mysterious chapter in life, which her child
had intended to put away for ever in the
lowest chamber of her mind, and never expose
to mortal handling. How cruelly she felt
wounded as she stood with the poisoned arrow
in her breast, shot by the only living creature
in the world to whom she might look for consolation in a family sorrow. Was she to have
imputations of frailty cast upon her because of
the whisper of a parent's wrong ?

" Uncle," she cried, her voice choking, "you
do not mean this ; it is not you who have
thought this cruelty, ay, this insult for me !
Who do you take me for ? have I then been

deceived in your kindness? I cannot remain with you longer when you suspect me of wrong."

The innate tenderness of her heart rushed upon her, and she leant for an instant to conceal her great sorrow; but quickly gathering her strength, she walked towards the door, intending to bid adieu to the place.

Oliver Arnot meanwhile, surprised at the power of his attack, recovered his true self and seized her hand. He cursed the imperfections of his language, and resolved to be silent ever on themes like these; he had tried the roundabout mode of attack, in which he had not succeeded, and now, flying to bluntness, he had mangled the object he desired to carry off in safety.

"O Ellen, Ellen! dinna be sae angry, I meant no insult, don't take it sae hotly; sit ye doun; you're no to leave this room till we be better friends than ever; just sit doun, and I promise ye amends."

Her face, as he led her back to a seat, wore an expression of severe pain.

"Ellen," said her uncle, moved to kindness; "I wish only it had been another, who's dead and gone, had been still living to care for ye. I'm no equal to it. Dr Lee was well-spoken and educated, but the best are ta'en first. Dinna be angry wi' me; it's the way o' doing things that makes the master. Jist ye say ye want nae mair o' this, and God help me, but I'll be dumb. Damn these clashing deevils," burst out the enraged farmer, casting upon the public the blame of his own unfortunate outbreak.

"I do not blame you, uncle, for warning me of what people say, nor for giving me your own best advice. They interfere with what does not concern them, and I know not how I have done wrong in your eyes."

"You've done nae wilful wrong, but just as a pretty lass canna help; though there's maybe danger and wrong to others. Says

auld Macalpine mony a year and day to me,
—his son would work till he made siller to buy
back the castle-lands, and get a richer lady for
his wife than he had done, or the auld curse o'
the family, pride and poverty, should level
them to the peasant's cot; he would be the
first to curse the son from the grave itsel', if
he were like the forbears. Ellen, if you 've no
gaen sae far as ye canna return, leave the son,
and brave not the anger of the mad laird, for
murder he would in his great moods. I hae
been to blame, lettin ye gae on; why didna I
stop ye at once? I take blame; dinna say
marriages are happy wi' difference o' condition.
Let the laird marry a lady, and the farmer a
farmer's daughter. There 's John Macpherson
o' the Mains, and an honest sonsy man, wi'
plenty bawbees, yoked wi' ane o' ten o' the puir
laird o' Girvan, and his life 's no worth living;
deil a thing but show; puir John himsel' noo
a mere bauble o' a creetur, wi' his money
aboot gane."

"You think, then," replied Ellen, "that I
will be a curse to this family if I remain longer
here. Better I had never been born than I
should come between any one and their happiness. In my simplicity I believed we had only
ourselves to heed. I have been mistaken ; let
me go and forget that I ever set my eyes on
Morven."

If a sacrifice was demanded of her, she
would silently set herself to the task. Her
belief and hope that Alan would deride the
notions of her uncle were strong. But would
the obstacle to their union not still be a true
one ? Were Alan's interests to be sacrificed
for her ? No ; she must go.

"Na, na; no that; you mustn't leave me,
Ellen ; my life has been happier wi' you in this
house than it has been for mony a year and
day. Ay, I 'm selfish enough to wish to keep
you ; but it 'll be for your ain gude i' the end.
Don't be low i' the spirits ; there 's twenty
men in the county 'll be after Ellen Lee, and

the niece of Oliver Arnot. Na, you mustna go."

" I want them not, uncle," broke in Ellen. " I will try and forget it all. I am sure you injure him terribly when you think he could be so base as to seek any woman's heart under the mask of love with the spirit of Mammon. Alan Macalpine is not such a one, I tell you," she repeated, her eyes flashing as she spoke. " Yet I must leave him. His world must not be mine. He will rise ; I would keep him down. The curse of his father neither he nor I must have."

But she was still under the tormenting spell of the sore which her uncle had goaded into the raw. At another time, she might have asked him boldly whether his words sprang from memory of her mother's conduct. She walked quickly out of the room, and Oliver Arnot was left to meditate upon the ill results of his diplomacy. He was exhausted with his morning's work. He went to his garden, and tried to dream himself into the belief that it was all right; that Alan would come as before; that his niece would be still merry in his hall, and that things would wag calmly into a ripe day, when his own shadow was no less than it was. But he rose to the chill air of the real prospect before him. His niece was not attending to the autumn flowers, as was her wont at this time, when he took his pipe; he sauntered slowly into the house, half-expecting that her clear voice would greet his ear. There was no sound there but the distant grating voices of the kitchen, among which stood out the commanding tones of his hard-voiced spouse.

Mrs Arnot, too, was herself excited all the morning. She recalled to her memory how she had known of women whose supposed affections had been severed from one object, greedily devour the next bait that presented itself. If her husband's niece saw herself torn from the side of Alan Macalpine, on account of family pride, might not she, in the rage and pet (which she, Mrs Arnot, thought she would feel), fall into the arms of her Tam.

Now, although Mr Thomas Scoular was not a good man,—indeed, he was a bad man, for he often indulged in the worst malignancy;— and although he was a dull stupid fellow at Finzean, while elsewhere he laughed and coarsely joked, and his brain was roused, and his heart moved, he was quite capable of appreciating the common types of beauty, and of contrasting with them his own coarse individuality. Since his mother had put into his ill-directed cranium thoughts of marriage with Ellen Lee, he had improved in his personal appearance; and when he was in the presence of Ellen, a softness, such as he never wore elsewhere, radiated his sandy face. Although animal throughout, he felt that in her there was a prize which it would be well to have. Neither did he see in her alone the heiress to his stepfather's wealth. There were humane sides of Thomas's advances to Ellen. The rest was blank and something worse. He felt abashed in the presence of modesty and virtue, and his speech to Ellen had been blundering and short; and now this morning he felt his hand tremble as he hung about the balustrades of the stair, expecting Ellen's approach after her interview with her uncle.

"Ellen, you're no lookin' weel," were the terms of Tom's accost, as she came down to where he stood. "Come in here and tell me what's wrang."

She looked up, surprised a little at such tones from this quarter.

"Not now, Tom; thank you, I'm not ill."

"But you are," said Scoular, obstinately. "Will you not do me a favour, Ellen. Tom Scoular has ever been your surest freend. Dinna be saucy noo."

Ellen looked at him, it almost seemed with a shudder, which she was able to conceal from him. She divined his intention, and, though not naturally timid, in her then situa-

tion of depression, she was for an instant afraid.
She wished it to appear that no breach of
good feeling had taken place, and cruel as the
task was, she entered into the parlour, the door
of which Scoular had ready open for her.

Scoular came to the point without beating
about as Oliver Arnot had done.

"Ellen, I love you. Dinna think that though
ye are your uncle's next o' kin I come to ye.
Ye'll mak' me a happy man as my wife;
that's why I ask ye to be 't. Maybe unlike
ithers I could name, I'm no a hand at fine
speeches, yet there's nane o' the hill sides hae
stronger hands to keep and protect ye than
me. A 'm joost what a 'm an' nae mair; an',"
—here he faltered, looking upon the unmoved
countenance of the woman he addressed. It
was cold, and her tongue speechless; very unlike this, the warm coarseness of the specimens
of the sex whose company he had best known.
"An' you 'se be weel cared for, without doot.
What ails ye, Ellen? If I were you, hang me,

but I'd come ower thae Macalpines. Joost
say the word, and I'll mittle Alan Macalpine
that no anither wummun i' a' Scotland or
England 'ither 'll look at the Hieland cock."

Ellen shuddered. Was this the man intended
for her? Was it that she might fall to his lot,
that those cruel demands had just been made
upon her by her uncle? The interview seemed
providential to drive her the quicker from the
house.

"Tom, you have deceived yourself; you
have not been encouraged to this by me. I
might have been your friend, but now——
Come to your better heart, and learn shame of
what you have now spoken."

Scoular stopped her progress as she advanced
towards the door, desirous to close the interview. He was almost speechless with savage-
ness, though not daring yet to lay hold
of her.

"Had thae been ither days, I'd made ye my
wife in spite o' ye."

"I thank God then," she answered, "who has made me in better days."

"You think me, I suppose, a puir man be- side Macalpine, and kick me aside; but no, lassie, I warn ye o' this wi' your airs o' gentry and spurn o' as gude bluid as runs in your veins. Come, noo, say ye were wrang to speak as ye've done."

"I will not say it; let me pass!"

"It's for Macalpine that maun ruin ye that ye refuse me."

"Let me pass," Ellen cried, pushing past him to the door handle.

"Ye'll no out here till ye say Tam Scoular's a better man than Alan Macalpine;" was the reply, laying hold of her arm.

"Never; coward, would you strike me?"

"Ay; murder ye, perhaps," in a half- humorous, half-diabolical growl.

"Let me go, or I'll alarm the house. I pity you, and will not speak of this," said the girl.

"Aff then, but damn your pride and his that

fells ye ; keep this to yersel', or the worse it 'll
be for ye and him." So growling he went out
first ; Ellen flying to her room to be alone—
alone, but not comfortless.

Tam Scoular stood in the passage with a face
on which anger was depicted to an unusual
degree even for him. His stepfather noticed
it, but said nothing, being in no mood for
speech with any one. It would be a quarrel
about money with his mother, thought Arnot,
knowing that these were of common occurrence.
Tam was seizing a large, broad, low-crowned
felt hat—which became well his harsh disagreeable features—as the other came into the passage, and with half-averted look stood for an instant as if hesitating whether he would speak
to Arnot. He, however, went quickly past him,
muttering in threatening tones, in which the
other could catch only, "Your niece 's a "——
"So then," thought the farmer to himself, "here
is insult to injury with a vengeance." He
groaned in spirit. He could have taken his

greatly loved niece to his arms and held her
back; he dared not now. He went about
that day distracted.

" Gone ! and the light gone with her, and left me in shadow
    here ;
Gone ! flitted away !
Taken the stars from the night and the sun from the day.
Gone ! and a cloud in my heart and a storm in the air ;
Flown to the east or the west, flitted I know not where."

CHAPTER VI.

OLIVER ARNOT wished to be only mysterious when Alan asked the circumstances which had taken Ellen away in his absence.

"O' nae doot; I ken she's weel; she'll turn up some fine day," was all the farmer would say, and Alan was obliged to rest content. He soon saw, however, that Ellen fled against her uncle's will, and when no explicit explanation came from Ellen herself, or any other, of the cause of her disappearance, Alan was deeply vexed by the thought that she had fled from himself. Oliver Arnot vaguely hinted that at all events his niece did not wish Alan to know her movements. "Why is this?" asked Alan, his voice shaking with indignation and pain. Oliver Arnot did not answer.

Months passed away, and all his efforts to

find out where Ellen had gone proved futile.
Her uncle hinted still that Ellen must pay
Finzean a visit in the summer, and that he
would then learn, from her own lips, what she
chose to tell ; and Alan was compelled to rest
content.

Meantime, the worthy farmer himself was
sore distressed at Ellen's absence, and with
himself, as the immediate cause of it. He
grew restless, and had again to seek refuge
outwith his own house, for occupation for his
idle hours. He had long ceased any regular
attendance at the village inn, for perusal of
the news, or a gossip with mine host, and
jabber with the frequenters of the tap-room ;
these habits he again felt necessary to kill
time, though the cellars of the Morven Arms
needed little more replenishing for the farmer's
visits.

Here, on an afternoon towards the close
of autumn, after a gloomy morning, when
the farmer had not before left his stead-

ing, and mine host was unusually slack for
want of the traveller who should still find his
way from the stage nearer town for his journey onwards through the strath, the reception
of Arnot was unusually cheerful.

"Ye 're late the nicht, Maister Arnot, and
here 's the hoose fou ! Just as I was at the
door twa hour syne, lookin' oot for the neeps
that should be here i' the mornin',—for thae
starvin' brutes o' horses that Captain Sykes has
put up,—up comes doucely, and speaks to me,
as if he had been nae mair than a tourist chap,
that taks to the road on the score o' health,
while his pouch 's only i' the death-thraw.
'Plenty o' rooms vacant i' your house, landlord ?' says he. 'Ay,' says I, 'mair than
there should be, considerin'.' 'Well, we shall
see,' he said, wi' the voice of General Farquhar,
and I saw a great gentleman he was—nae a
halflin chap wi' claes he pretends, an' finer
than their wearer ; so in he gaes, looks at five
rooms, and taks them for a week. An, puir

man, he 's taen na mair denner than serves a
flea ; a bit steak, a bit bread, an a thimlefu o'
best cognac. But the rascals o' men—twa he has
—cam an hour after wi' luggage ; that a ay
care ta see, come o' the handsomeness o' the
owner what likes. Oh, but he 's auld and
tired-lookin, but a real ane. But here'st,
Maister Arnot—the bell rings, and here he 's
lyin' on twa chairs, wi' his een glarin' like a
tiger's oot o' a jungle. 'Can you tell me of a
farmer hereabouts who knows the land ? ' he
asks. What 's up noo, thinks I ; maybe ye 'r
a government man, though I said naething o'
this ; maybe a painter we read o', that gets
hunders for bits o' picters ; or an author ; but
na, nane o' that, I 'll reckon, wi' five rooms,
and twa idle dogs worryin i' the kitchen.
Ye 're after Morven estate ; though I said
naething o 't, but just this, that Maister Oliver
Arnot kent best aboot the land i' the haill
coonty. There it is, the lang an' the short o 't.
I said, ' Sir, Maister Arnot 's been on 's farm

ever syne Roderick Macalpine focht the duel wi' the young Englishman, and that's no yestreen, as ye, sir, may learn frae himsel'; here he wheezed, and looked hard at me. And noo, sir, as I may be doin' ye a gude turn, just, Maister Arnot, do me anither,—keep them at it—that we may draw mair o' the auld Macalpine claret, that's ower lang i' the cellar; and the stories 'll be gude for yoursel, that will sit sae douce thae months back."

Arnot was now ushered in upon the stranger. It was already dusk, and a cheerful, blazing fire, which the constitution of the lodger seemed to demand, gave to his thin, bronzed, and somewhat haggard features, an unusual tinge of warmth. His years were probably not sixty. Whether from the habitual working of strong passions, or from a life spent in an unhealthy climate, or perhaps from both causes, his frame was attenuated, and his expression that of a man of greater age. A keen observer would have detected in his smallest movement indications of a mind indifferent to the common pleasures of the world. A certain elevation of mind still could pierce through the stillness of the face. Yet all was not well in that heart; success appeared upon the brow, but the dim, troubled eye, and the drawn-up cheek, portrayed that that success had brought not peace; it had come whence he cared not to think over to himself. The manners of the stranger were quiet and gentlemanly. He gave no trouble; everything was done as he wished it; the force he possessed being the actual outcome of a naturally determined and fearless character. Arnot was soon taken with the agreeable intercourse. The quick, hurried, and often boisterously important guests of the inn, whether they were of the low or high rank of the traveller of pleasure or necessity, were not much to the taste of the worthy farmer. Here was a gentleman who, at once and without any effort, placed himself on the level with his visitor. Yet he appeared deep, quiet, and historical, such as the true man of the world is.

"Sir Andrew Cameron informs me that a large property is for sale here—the estate of Morven—Macalpine's lands; and I wish a practical man to advise me of the capacity of the farms," said the stranger.

"Sir Andrew himself will be a better judge o' that than I am," answered the farmer. "He kens the value o' every knowe i' the county. An' then ye see, I'm a tenant o' Morven, and maybe if ye were laird ye might tak' me at my ain estimate, which is low enough aboot Finzean—my ain place—for the laird's needfulness gat me to gie a high rent, an' wi' that an' the drouth o' the past twa years I've lost siller,"—grumbling half-humorously to his prospective landlord, with the certain instincts of a tenant-farmer. "But for a' that I'll no say that I dinna ken the land, ditch an' hill-tap, pasture an' bog, an' the sheep and cattle that they'll keep. So be't ye tak' me wi' a' fauts, I'm happily at your service."

Next day, by appointment, Arnot waited

upon the sojourner at Morven Inn, who then introduced himself as Colonel Mar, and both proceeded to Morven Castle, with the view of commencing there some inspection of the property. It was a dull day of autumn ; one of those days which seem to be forecast with the shadow of the coming winter. The darkening melancholy of the clouds, spread in inert masses over the whole sky ; the fitful winds, raising the sough of the boughs of the forest trees; the murmurs and twitterings of the leaves of the beech and birch ; the fall of the heavy leaf of the oak and plane, in the intervals of stillness; the yellow melancholy sitting upon all nature, —were not without their influence upon the mind of Colonel Mar. The precincts of the Castle all bore the mark of a poor proprietorship, decayed from a position which had often indulged habits of expense and a taste for splendour. Dear as had been the pride of their lands to all of them, the Macalpines had had no practical value for them. Nature had

been bountiful with the beauty indestructible ;
art had been exercised to heighten effects, and
comfort had not been forgotten ; but increase
of value there was none commensurate with
the outlay. The pillared and arched gateway
bore upon each pinnacle, in excellently chiselled
stone-work, the crest of the Macalpines, while
neglect marked every ' feature of the parks
around. The walks of the avenue were, as
was to be expected, overgrown with weeds
where the dense coverings of leaves, blown by
the winds, left here and there a bare spot of the
ground ; bushes hung over upon the roadway,
and nestled their heads deep in the body of
decaying matter. Towards the castle the trees
grew high and broad, forming a contrast to
the drooping life around them. A massive
tower, which shot up from amidst a series of
more modern-looking erections, was the distinguishing feature of the castle from a distance,
and gave it an imposing appearance, beauti-
fully situated as it was, upon an eminence of

considerable dimensions, which looked down
upon the pebbly stream of Morven, and far
over the strath to the distant mountain-tops.
The companion of Oliver Arnot paused as he
came within sight of the castle, but the farmer
was too intent upon his own thoughts of the
ruin of the Macalpines, to notice the effect upon
the other of the silent story of decay. A
flushed face, a brightness in the troubled eye,
and a quickness in the step, changed for an
instant the worn man into a youth,—as if he
recalled ambitious fire into his veins as it
burned when hope lives in the realms of an
imagined existence,—as Colonel Mar stepped
through a path which diverged from the main
avenue, and brought them to an arbour scene,
from which autumnal splendour had not yet
altogether fled. Through a maze or thicket
was an enclosure formed of trees of many
varieties, whose leaves blended all the richness
of an Oriental colouring : in the space grew
the most luxuriant flowers of autumn, upon

which seemed to travel for a moment, through the rising masses of the glowing foliage of the trees, the rays of a gleaming sun. It might have been the deception of the colours as the scene first burst upon the vision, for it appeared to Colonel Mar, as he awoke from what was a short reverie, that nature stood in gloom.

"A bonnie place, but bluid has been spilt there," said the farmer, who had to wait his companion's exit.

"How, man, how?" inquired Colonel Mar, eagerly, belying the former dignified quiet of his manner.

"Oh, nae murder! there's nae ghosts to frighten yer young folk i' the winter nichts. Just the duel that Dougal maybe told ye o'."

"No doubt some legend, scarcely founded on fact."

"Fact it is, Colonel Mar; that in this place Roderick Macalpine took some bluid oot o' a young Englishman wha challenged him for

running off with his sweetheart, then laird
Macalpine's wife."

"How did she live, then, with this wild
Highland chief—this English lady?"

"But I haven't told you how it cam' aboot.
Roderick was a dashing fellow in his young
days, and broken as he is, has a fine eye wi'
the women; gentle in his way wi' them,
though a cursed temper wi' maist men. Tak'
care, Colonel, hae as little business as ye can
wi' him; I that shouldna' say 't that am weel
and hearty wi' him. Weel, Macalpine the
laird, as he was just then, was at Bath, on his
way home from London, and he fancied a
gentle English lass that he met there, that
was a' but bein' married to a young English
officer, as they said; no that she was 'trothed
to him in form, but it was aye said it was an
understood thing between them, and amang
kith and kin; ah! but the laird was the finest
man o' the ball-room,—danced with the lord-
liest fling aboon a' the nobility o' the land

congregated at the ball, an' he spoke to the leddies o' the romance o' his native land, and rhymed a ballad or twa ; and, Lord help them, but their fancies were quite wild wi' him,— and the supposed heiress, false or no " ——

" False, certainly, if actually betrothed by word or implication," broke in the other, with some sternness.

" Weel, I 'll no say false ; for as fine, gentle, and kind a leddy never was kent. The laird filled her heart fou, and off she cam wi' him to Morven, taking the blacksmith to marry them on the road. Off starts the lieutenant and misses them,—he was here before them ; and Tam Cameron tells yet o' the loud knock o' the infuriate Southerner, begging your pardon, Colonel, as he got to the castle gate. Then comes the pair to Morven,—the laird, restless and willsome, as he is in all his ways, walked alone in advance up to the castle ; and here, just as we come oot, springs the Englishman upon him, and strikes him wi' his sword. The

Macalpines were aye ready to return, and
gettin' to the arbour, where he was provided
wi' a weapon, they foucht. The men heard
the clashing o' swords as they cam' up, a
quarter o' an hour after; an' my leddy, catching that somethin' was wrang, flew in upon
them an' fainted, but no until the Englishman
had a deep wound which lasts him yet, if
he's i' the world; he fell there in a pool o' his
ain makin'; the warld, nae doot, played him
ill. Gude be wi' him if he was wranged, and
gi'e him better luck with the next woman,—
though heaven be praised, my passions ne'er
took me gaen daft after ane when there are
sae mony o' them on the braid earth."

"What became, then, of this English lover?"

"He was as wild as the laird in his ain
fashion. Had the laird been so used, he would
hae pulled doun the castle aboot his enemy's
lugs. This young callant just muttered, as he
was borne off, that Macalpine's bluid would
yet join his ain in feedin' the lands o' Morven

when they were no more his ; thinkin' o' the
rhyme he had read maybe that mornin' :—

> " ' Macalpine's bluid will freeze like wine,
>   When Morven Castle he shall tyne.'

" But it goes on—

> " ' Macalpine's heir will get his ain,
>   Ere that lost bluid can run again.'

"There were them that saw him at the inn,
while he rested, that said Macalpine might look
out for a reckonin'.   They said he looked as if
they hadna seen the last o' him, like auld
Dundee, when he damned the lords of Con-
vention he couldna control."

" And the lady, how did she fare with the
hare-brained Highlander ? "

" No hare-brained, Colonel ; just wild and
high tempered.   Roderick Macalpine has had
a fine head, though it 's no just aye sound, nae
mair than half the world's is."

" But I need not ask," broke in Colonel Mar,
interrupting the speaker, not having listened
to his last remark ; "what could the gentle

spirit of this lady, bred in the happy peace of a true English home, have in common with such a man. Had she been a common specimen of woman-kind she would not have been the victim of this fellow. Once her senses fell to the level of the life around her I doubt not she was awakened to a feeling of remorse, and saw in its real colour the vain love of Macalpine. The bloom of the English rose upon her cheek must in little time have degenerated to the thin pallor of your starved wild one. To transplant the gayest flower of our garden to your storm-beaten hill, is no less attended with certain destruction, than the transplanting to its men the daughters of the sunny south. Proudly it seems to wed the towering Loch-na-gar, but its embrace is the embrace of death ; and the tender daughter of England seeks her doom in alliance with the cateran descendant of the hills," said Colonel Mar, bitterly.

"I'm thinkin' the comparison's no fair," replied the farmer. "If the ane's too strong, the ither's too gentle at that rate; the vine 'll no grow here, but ye 'll admit, Colonel, the mountain dew 's no ill substitute, though a drap o' water doesna droon the miller. I 'm no for mixtures, but it strikes me a Highland laird 's no ill match for ony English lass, let her be wha likes, an' if the country be ower cauld for her—why, let her stay at hame."

"But if she be seduced."

"I never knew ane seduced. If the lass prefers a strappin' Hieland chief to a tame creepin' English boddie, wha is there to say she 's wrang, though her husband's temper ance o' the week mounts as high as Ben-Nevis."

"Well, my good friend," answered Colonel Mar, "we are not to quarrel in our argument. I was wrong to include your whole Highlands in my anathema; but touching this Roderick Macalpine, whom heaven make as good a man as nature allows him to become,—did he cherish the woman he bore off from the south? You

interest me deeply in the fortunes of the beings
that dwelt here."

"Truth to tell, many a time hae I seen her
staun' and sigh here, on this very spot. Macalpine was no ill to her, for he ever was the
gentleman, every inch; but he neglected her,
if it be cherishing ye ask after. Her boy wasna
born till a good six years after the marriage;
that was a misfortune. The laird was every
day fou' o' schemes for which his wife cared no
a bodle. One day he had discovered a compost
to bring double craps oot o' the land, and he
would have me to try 't, which I did wi' half
a dozen acres o' the best arable, but deevil a
thing would grow, weeds as aits were burned
oot o' the earth; then water was to be drawn
frae the clouds i' the dry weather; sugar was
to be made frae sawdust, an' a' the trees were
cut and manufactories put up, but after a' expense I 've ne'er seen a pickle sugar, sae muckle
as sweeten a cup o' tea; an' then when things
were a' wrang, he quarrels wi' the next laird

aboot the marches, wi' bondholders aboot their interest, wi' an uncle about an auld family provision ; though Macalpine himsel' aye throve upon a' his wark sae far as the body went, his good lady pined upon the hard fare, and lived no mony years. She was sadly forfouchten wi' the laird, I'll no deny."

"Her soul rests in peace, which it had not done here," exclaimed the other, who listened dreamily to the voluble farmer.

The two now were admitted to the castle by an old crone who had sole charge of the place. The old family furniture, the gatherings of generations, was also for disposal; the whole property, heritable and movable, real and personal, wheresoever situated, according to the phraseology of Scotch law, being in the market. The estate was unentailed, and the last proprietor had completed the havoc of reckless ownership, all that really remained for his sustenance being some small means which had belonged to his wife.

"Saw ye ever the like, Maister Arnot!"
burst out the abigail, as the party was admitted into the hall, almost dying to hear her
voice, which, of recent weeks, had evidently
languished for its accustomed exercise. "Here
hae been the laird an' Maister Rab Munro,
fechtin' the haill mornin'. Mercy, gentlemen,
I'm no the laird's wumman or I'd stand the
collyshangy, but I'm lonely here, an' anither
maun be got to keep the place warm ; ye may
see 't, gentlemen, the day, but gin I'm livin'
the morn I canna be here ; there's ghaistly
soonds enou a' the eirie nicht, let alane the
mornin', when folk should be happy an' pleased
like. But the laird comes in,—he that I wasna
to let in without the writer,—an' then he
stood an' he jumped, an' he stamped wi' his
feet, an' damned to hell-fire the haill regiment
o' lawyers, an' then he strides up the ha' an' I
says, 'D'ye ken, laird, my orders werena to let
ye in syne the place was taen frae ye, beggin'
yer lairdship's pardon for bein' sae bold—I,

that was a puir wumman, an' had her week's wages; an' then he luckies me, an' scowls at me, an' staps a shillin' i' my han', an' swore he kent ma faither, an' saw me half-an-hoor efter I was born; I that am—weel, maybe a year or twa—aulder than himsel'; but in comes Maister Rab Munro, an' they steekit an' they foucht for near an hoor afore they moved oot i' hall. Heerd ye, gentlemen, ever o' papers they ca' Seasons, Wadsets, Backbanes, Dispensations, an' Chatters o' Nicodemus? for the clatter they got up about sic like things wad deave a mad-hoose; beggin' yer pardon, gentlemen, for keepin' ye stannin', but gin ye fin' me deaf-like, jist put it doun to the din I heard; an' gin ye fin' me hoarse an' ill at the speakin', its nae for tire o' the travellin' o' the tongue, for faith, sirs, I may address the deevil here."

"This indicates differences between Mac-alpine and any purchaser of his lands," remarked Colonel Mar to Arnot.

"Deed, sir, ye say true," remarked the abigail. "The laird had an armfu' o' auld musty parchments he got oot o' a tin box that lay i' the garrets ; an' gin he canna lay aboot the lugs o' the incomer wi' sic a load o' law, he 'll no be the man I tak' him for."

"Why, Mistress Meg," said the farmer, "ye 're an ill servant o' the bondholders, that begins wi' showin' the black side o' the security lands. Na, na ! I 'll warrant a' richt, or the laird 'd been here this day. Gin there be a letter oot o' the richt place in the parchments, he 'd mak the Court o' Session ring wi' the news."

"I canna vouch for what the laird may dae, or onybody dae," said Meg.

"I fear, Meg," said the farmer, jocosely, as the crone tripped beside his portly person, "ye canna get ower the laird's flattery, pretty fellow as he is."

"Did ye ever hear the like ?" cried the pock-marked Meg, her complexion and eyes brightened to an age twenty years younger, and leaping off to the Colonel like a coquette of nineteen summers. "Weel, an' I waur as I was ance on a day, deil hae 't, but Laird Macalpine micht hae burned the hoose aboot my lugs, and I wudna run for a wat blanket."

The interior of the mansion bore the same evidences as without of the decayed circumstances of its owner, The numerous rooms were in disorder, that no Meg Ramage might be expected to repair. Fine oaken cabinets, chairs and couches, antique-looking as the Urquhart family itself, were piled and choked with boxes and heaps of print and manuscript, and the floors themselves of several of the rooms were scarcely accessible beyond the doors, except by wading and fording through this labyrinth of trash and disorder. These collections were the monuments of Macalpine's former cherished designs, and ill-fated pleas-in-law. Portraits of the family of Macalpine for many generations were there, seemingly to be disposed of as cheaply as Charles Surface knocked down those of his ancestors to his uncle Sir Oliver. Among these stood conspicuous the portraits of Roderick Macalpine and his wife.

"These, too, are seized," exclaimed Colonel Mar. The haughty form and features of Macalpine looked disdain from his picture upon the attenuated man who now gazed upon it ; who returned with a double scorn—of which the slight animation in his face was no index—the haughtiness of the portrait, as he turned to the other, representing a lady of rather more than the middle height, dressed in the fanciful garb with which the sitters for a portrait used to be adorned. The effect upon Colonel Mar was at once to charm away the ill effect of his gaze upon the other. The portrait was evidently one at which the artist had worked in his best humour ; he had given to the canvas the distinguishing animation of expression which is one of the most difficult attainments of the brush. The feminine softness

of the mouth, and the tender intelligence of the
eyes,—arched by such brows as might have inspired the sonnets to that feature which poets
are supposed to delight in,—were, with a
shapely and fresh cheek, characteristics of a
portrait which represented a lady possessing a
lively fascination. Not yet had the eye
dimmed, or the mouth compressed, or the
cheek paled; not yet did she feel bereft of
the love she lived on; not yet had she
found neglect, and recognised that there was
no returning from the course she had chosen
in her gay dalliance, and that only must she
seek, in the care of her child and the sympathy
of the not unfeeling hearts of the tenantry, a
solace for her wounded love.

Leaving the castle of the Macalpines,
Colonel Mar and his companion drove over
portions of the estate. Places of interest, connected with history or local legend, or afford-
ing views of grand scenery, were in turn
visited, and though Colonel Mar made many

inquiries and examinations as to the quality of the soil and pasturage and the extent of the game, it was evident he regarded these matters as of secondary importance. It seemed, at all events, that after his visit at the castle, he had made up his mind to become a bidder for the property, and its owner.

The day had become duller and more cheerless. The single smile of sunlight that had irradiated the scene for an instant seemed to bear, to Colonel Mar, as it never returned, some prophecy of the opening career of his intended new life as a landlord of a noble property. This was not the buoyant birth anticipated of years, but a sickly abortion.

CHAPTER VII.

THE interest manifested about Morven consequent upon a change in the proprietorship of the estate was intensified, to the gossips and the politicians of the village, by the frequently repeated question of, "How 'll Macalpine take it?" There were parties and lively divisions in the tap-room of the Morven Arms the night before Colonel Mar's arrival as the proprietor of the estate. One headed by Macnab the tailor, who had visions in the new household of wardrobes, of which the old had for long had a limited supply, talked of common sense, and bespoke good-will for the new-comers who had injured no one, and would do the place "mair gude than a ranting laird." "It was notorious," so said the tradesman, "that auld Macalpine was not a man of the age, but a Highlander of the last century, who could take but could never give except fight."

Cameron, the game-dealer, led the party who sided with "the owner who had gone down." He stigmatised the tailor and his lot,—yet so good-humouredly as not to hazard their continued patronage as purchasers of poached hares,—as turncoats and worshippers of the rising sun.

"The auld laird was as gude," argued the old poacher, "as he was forty years syne, when the haill village was at his back, and he should never want a hare or a muirfowl sae lang as his feet could crush stubble or his legs carry ower the heather. And what's mair," continued the generous man, becoming prophet, "we'll see the laird back in his ain; the Macalpines were aye sib wi' Providence at their last gasp. An' here's tae Roderick, lord of Morven, for a' that."

The toast was drunk with applause; though most shook their heads, some yet with the

shake of half belief ; and it came to be accepted
among the credulous that auld Macalpine had
a scheme which would prove sufficient to restore him, though the estate had gone from
him by lawful purchase.

It is in the soul of women to demand attraction.   The masculine spirit of Portia was
feminine in this, that she was determined to
be loved.   So under apparent indifference in
Lucretia Mar's force of character, dwelt this
passion of her sex.   The best sleeping apart-
ment of Morven had been set apart for her,
and lying there on the morning after her
arrival in luxurious restlessness, her thoughts
wandered from the grandeur of the scene which
the uncurtained window revealed, to imaginations of its native heroes, whose devotion, all
strange and romantic, might be hers, and open
to her the realities of love, the richest fruit of
the garden of the world, of which she had never
tasted.

"Madge," she said to the maid who disturbed her reverie, "I grow a believer in your Highlands; I am romantic, and have been dreaming of a castle and its hero devoted to me like a slave. I must go in search of adventure. You have got bottomless lochs and endless caverns, haunted castles and warlock glens,—surely some hero will assert himself; have you no grand specimens like your mountains, or are your men mere commonplace pigmies?"

Madge was a lowland Scotchwoman of shrewd and intelligent character, who had passed her youth at Morven, and was quickly a favoured domestic attached to its new mistress, whose familiarity she had courted without abusing it.

"'Deed, my lady, they're not pigmies, big handsome fellows that can hurl stones as big as I am."

The lady laughed, and lay back on her pillow, listening, however, to the continued chat of her maid, as she related some local histories bearing on the glories of the late lords of Morven, and with great tact contriving to introduce something more than the name of its last heir. Now and again the occupant of the couch stretched forth, with a sort of weary energy, a hand of delicate colour, but of more than woman's fibre, and her dark eye gave a sign of interest as anything singular in the gossip struck her mind. As her maid put the last finish to the adornment of the folds of her black luxuriant hair, she turned to Madge with a moment's curiosity, and asked—

"How old is this chief, the heir of Macalpine, of whom you have been babbling?"

"I'll warrant him as young as he's handsome, with a heart as frank as a mountain daisy that has ne'er known the wiles of the south wind," answered Madge.

"That is to say," rejoined the lady, "though he is a hero, his cold, chaste heart must succumb to the warmth of southern beauty."

"Just so, Lady Lucretia, though it's not

many gentle folks either that'll please the proud Macalpine."

"Indeed! he is a noble, then. In what castle does the family now support its dignity?" asked Miss Mar.

"Alas! in no castle; Morven was their last; their worldly gear is low at this hour, but faith, my lady, Alan Macalpine is a braw man for learning, and he'll make the world stir yet with sword or pen or the eloquence of the Parliament."

"You remind me of Caleb Balderston, Madge, and your chief something of Ravenswood, but I fear there will be no Lucy Ashton. Ladies do not fall in love now with ruined men, outlaws from society, and I fear this Macalpine has only his pride and a few family portraits to support him. Is there no member of the Peerage whose estates lie by, with one or more sons, such as we saw on landing at our last stage by the coach—these were noblemen and men of estates."

"Heigho! my lady, they are all that to look at; but if ye had spoken to them you would have heard nothing else than about horses and cock-fights. My lady, excuse my heat; ye got me to come from Lady Barnton's to your ladyship, and I ne'er was gladder; nothing but fighting, eating, and drinking, frae morn to night. The Mars are a great folk, and will ken the Macalpines when they see them—far awa frae the cock-fighting and horse-racing gentry."

CHAPTER VIII.

THE sale of Morven by the creditors had been hastened by the instrumentality of Alan Macalpine, whose shrewd common sense had hailed the opportunity of extricating his father from his difficulties, by the disposal of it to Colonel Mar at a sum which many in the county regarded as something fabulous. The elder Macalpine felt the alienation keenly, especially at the moment that the stranger entered his familiar gate and took possession of the old family domain.

"This is the most damning day of all my life," he cried ; "my property—my god of this earth—taken from me for ever, kills me. Alan, do you think there can be no flaw about all this? Why were you not a lawyer? We might have checkmated them yet. If we could see but a flaw somewhere, there might

be a hope." The tear stood in the eyes of the
fallen stalwart chief, as he looked forth upon the
trees which bordered the way to his old mansion, and protected it from the winds. They
were alive again, freshening in their bright
green, in the growing spring, to deck the
environs of their new owner.

Alan waited a calmer moment for his opportunity to refer to their new situation, consequent upon the arrival of the new proprietor
of Morven. Preferring rather to discuss a
painful subject in the quiet starry night, than
by the dull candle light of a small room, which
contrasted strongly with Morven, he met his
father at the door, returning from an evening
walk. "I've got news for you—news that I
haven't known the marrow of for many a
day," was the father's greeting, as he stood at
his door. Alan thought little of this, except
that he was pleased with the old man's
pleasure. The elations of his father were fre-
quent, and therefore often about marvellously

small things. Roderick Macalpine stood in considerable awe of the calm, judicious, reasonable temper of his son; and Alan appreciated, with liveliness, the better side of his father's character; though he had learned much to guide himself by the sad wreck which his father had made of his life and property. He loved the unworldliness of the high-tempered and heroic Highlander. The adventurous spirit of the laird in his younger days was still the subject of talk in the district, to which he had in his boyhood listened with pleasure. He saw that failure in life had arisen from playing with it—playing, certainly often, with ugly-looking weapons, rather than seizing it with the bull-dog obstinacy and aggression, by which the determined man wins his way to success, and yet, often fails utterly in reaching happiness.

While the father's activity was loud and showy, the habits of his son, as we have partly seen, were inclined to the contemplative.

Nature had bestowed upon him a keen sensibility, which his situation, and a shrewdness common to an inheritance of blood both Saxon and Scotch, had ripened into some fruit. In early youth the cotter, the labourer, the shepherd, the ploughman, " who homeward wend their weary way," formed much of his society ; passing nights beside their rude, but seldom cheerless or boorish hearths. Years and education had developed early attachment into a sterner sympathy, and he had done them some service, while he was eager to effect a great rise in the condition of the peasantry. With an intensity, increased by a study of the French philosophers of the Revolution, the influence of which was great upon the fervid mind of a youth already acquainted with misfortunes, and accustomed to solitude in the bracing regions of the Grampians, he deplored the inequalities he saw around him, and though the springs of his heart would have led him to rest upon the past, he began to believe only in the future. He burned keenly with the hope that the meagrely-provided sons of toil should rise a noble race of educated men, while retaining all the simpleness of life which he believed to be the best suited to all men's happiness. One of the consequences of this feeling was, that the family pride of Macalpine became to him a myth; it and his own sorrows were nought in the presence of the poverty and the depression he saw at his side, and of his ardent hopes of changing the want or the misery to a solid happiness. So strong had been the tenderness of his spirit of justice, that his common enjoyments were often damped by the reflection of the inability of others to procure the like.

But while Alan was no sentimental or wild enthusiast—rather a practical Scottish gentleman, whose romance only appeared in the business of life to promote its just movement— the direction of his thoughts was gall and wormwood to his father, who, while he recognised

in these something at which, in his secret heart
and at its best moments, he felt a tinge of
pride, saw in them the ruin of his decaying
hopes. Instead of a son devoted with passion
to all the memories of the past, and eagerly
bent on pursuing the road to wealth and distinction, hoping to restore his house, it might
be, with double honours; here was a youth
who seemed to despise such feelings, while
he bent his energies towards redeeming the
situation of men whom he, Roderick, had
always looked upon, though he treated them
kindly, as the mere slaves of his will.

Not till to-day had the reality of his position,
and the connection with it of his own sins,
struck Roderick with that dull thud, comparable
only to the stroke of the wave which tells the
doom of the stranded and ill-guided vessel. He
had gone forth and found forgetfulness, as was
his custom, in the conviviality of simple volu-
bility of speech; on this occasion, as it happened, with Wat McTavish, who had introduced

the subject of the new arrival at Morven, and,
finding the laird attentive, had told all the
gossip concerning Colonel Mar and his daughter.
The laird, when it was possible, was quick with
any scheme which he might suppose to be ad-
vantageous to his own fortunes. He bore off in
excitement a plan of marrying his only son to
the daughter of the new proprietor, and thus
securing the estate to the old family. She was
represented by McTavish to be a young, handsome, and dashing woman, desiring to increase
her knowledge and love of the Highlands, which
were new and strange to her, and disposed to
look upon the chiefs of the clans as heroes of
romance. But the remembrance of the son's
unimpulsive character chilled the ardour of the
father, as he plodded on over the rugged roadway, and reduced his walk to a trudge from
the high step with which he had set out on
his return ; and now as he reached the house
and told of the plan, Alan was struck with the
faltering way he threw out the words which

had, as Alan thought, but a few minutes before
been coined in his heart's core.

"Father," he said, as the old Highlander
paused, hesitating while unfolding his latest
project of aggrandisement, "let us go away
from Morven to-morrow ; it will be better for
you that we leave it."

"Never, Alan ! never will I desert the home
of my fathers. It is no longer mine, but the
old hills are there, and the river ; they cannot
take the sight of these from me. Oh ! the old
bones would rattle i' the kirkyard, and plague
me with dreams, that I should sleep no more,
like the regal murderer, if I ran away from the
old lands."

"I love them as you do," said the son, "and
their people too, but you are tearing your heart
with the touch of them. Do not say I am
an Englishman in my feelings, and that I wish
to settle in the country of my mother, though
it would not be unnatural if I did, could you
but bring your mind to come with me. I am a

Scotchman to the backbone as you are, and here
I will remain with you and the country side
if my duty lies so. Yet we are living in the
shadow only of our former selves, forcing ourselves to it out of love and pride. For your
own health's sake, leave Morven ; sacrifice our
love for our urgent need.

"Do you think I am afraid to meet the
rabble crowd that will look down upon me
now, or that I'll creep aside on the highway
when the new lord of Morven honours it with
his equipage. Damn them, Alan ! a Macalpine
may lose his lands, but never the stout heart
that was born of its soil."

The son applauded the last sentiment. The
mere sentiment of the father was always real.

"I am getting older, but I am young enough
to look after myself. You are free, my boy, to
choose your own career. Mine lasts its time
beside the heather. You must seek your fortune now, after we are wound up, in the land
of gold, if you do not get a wife with a fortune,

and the old lands of Morven will come back
again—

> "'When Morven Castle he shall tyne,
> Macalpine's heir will get his ain,'

before my hairs are too white to trust them to
the winter winds."

The father paused, thinking that now he
might excite his son to resolve to pursue this
night the course of fortune-seeking he had laid
before him often enough in some guise or other.

"If you remain, I remain!" was all the son
said.

"You are too unambitious," said Roderick,
with a little anger.

"I have no ambition to grow by the foul
beds of injustice and oppression. You forget
the villany of Indian adventure; the strong
crush the life's blood out of the weak, that they
may come home and gratify their selfish pride.
But I won't think that our neighbour has had
service with the devil."

"For the sake of his daughter," ejaculated

the laird; "I would myself be interested in this happy heiress of Morven, were not my limbs bent," he continued solemnly; breaking away into his humorous sallies, sadly forced as these were to begin with.

"Think you not," answered the son, "she would ask where your other estates lay, and discovering none, would resent the presumption?"

The laird now got into a state of humour, droll in its torrent, which set all rational discussion at defiance.

"Presumption! do you think me such a fool that I should put it in the power of a woman to sully my honour, and that woman the daughter of a nabob. By heaven, sir, you wrong your father to conceive the possibility of such a thing. I should deserve to be carted to the gallows after being horsewhipped till half-dead—I should be deprived of the name of man, if I begged of a woman like this, to be whistled down the wind. My name and my

clan are enough—sufficient to outweigh every
ounce of Indian gold. I should march to her
a conquering hero; she could not refuse me,
nor could she you."

Roderick had forgotten, till his breath was
out, all about his intended scheme of marrying
his son to the daughter of the nabob. The
indulgence of his humour came in the way.

But for all he had said to furnish his son with
a retort, he might readily have turned round,
had not the opportunity been brought to an
end by the approach of a man whom they distinguished as Wat McTavish himself.

Wat was a farmer for a few years, and failed
to retain his lands on account of failure to pay
his rent, a misfortune he never ceased wholly
to attribute to the destruction of his crops by
game, and to an attempt at law to obtain redress,
a process which languished on his side by the
formidable opposition of Sir Andrew Cameron,
his landlord. Having received a fair education,
he became a schoolmaster, retaining more than

his former fondness for destroying ground game, if not also sporting on the moors. He was a smart, dapper little fellow, with red cheeks, very unlike the traditional dominie.

"You're not going to leave Morven, Mr Alan; I'm right glad o' that," said Wat to Alan as he came up.

"Ah! my lad, you'll have a harder man to deal with than Roderick Macalpine," said the laird.

"Weel, laird, I'll say this, that though you have been hard on your neighbour lairds, you've never been but kind to the puir."

"Puir! the last time I was i' the schule-hoose twa hares, half a dozen rabbits, and a brace of muir-fowl were hanging for the pot."

"Wheesht, laird, ye mind weel ye lunched next day aff the soup. The hare was nane the waur though it had tasted the Morven tubers."

"Deevil tak' ye, if he hasna ye already. Mind I'm a justice o' the peace yet; I'll hae ye up. I'm keeping in with Andrew Cameron,

and he'd part wi' his right hand to get ye i'
the lock-up."

"He'll no part wi' his siller, and the auld
process cost him ower much. They say, laird,
that ye'll be sune back, so we'll no hae lang
to wait for a free shot on Morven."

"I'll never be back, Wat, except Alan there
gets the lands; but he won't leave his
father," said Roderick, restored to reasonable
humour.

"To win fame and fortune," interrupted
Wat.

"I have no desire for fame or fortune,"
Alan observed slowly, gazing into the night,
scarcely knowing whether to be angry or pleased
at the moment with the varying humours of
the laird; "I am happy without either. It's
a depraved passion, the common seeking after
wealth, much more in my estimation than that
for destroying muirfowl, and I fear I should
be only like my neighbours if I sought it. Do
you believe, Wat, that after a terrible struggle

for wealth, I would allow you, and such as you, to trespass on it. I know the flesh too well." Alan spoke with little fervour; his thought was intenser.

"Good heavens, Alan!" cried his father, "you are an epicure, after a fashion. But wait till you are my age for the verdict on life without money-bags."

"I'm right glad o' this," cried Wat. "It takes no muckle logic to convince me that Mr Alan Macalpine should stay in Morven, e'en though I bag fewer hares by the stay, and though maybe ye keep doun my pouch a wee bit by taking in the lads to the school-house i' the winter. But it's the cotter-women that cry out they'd miss ye," continued he, slily, determined to have some little retaliation upon young Macalpine, who had spoken with severity of his poaching exploits.

The old laird of Morven got cheery again in the company of the schoolmaster and poacher, and Wat had a bowl of the "barley bree" in the

Lodge of the Macalpines, where he discoursed withal " science popularly explained."

Alan was of course sincere to his heart's core, in believing that his perfect duty was being accomplished ; and who will say that it was not ?

The poet has a land, even in the most circumscribed space, which is not of the world —far, hazy, retreating—the blue mountain peak, and the shadowy valley draped by the evening cloud, where imagination travels—a land scarcely reached, and never penetrated.

CHAPTER IX.

MUCH of the work of improvement at Morven
Castle began upon the arrival of the new proprietor. Before his coming with his daughter,
Colonel Mar had, indeed, set at work numerous
hands to make the old castle comfortable, and
the surrounding grounds trim ; and he would
have sat down content with what had been
accomplished. Not so his daughter. Her
bustling active temper was never to be satisfied without great ongoings, and her appreciation of what had been done by no means
corresponded with that of her father. She was
determined that a contrast should as quickly
as possible manifest itself to all between the
ruin of the late owner, and the substance and
luxury of the present one. It was a pleasure
to her to make old things new, to resuscitate,

and out of her energy and wealth bring the ancient out with a new sheen.

Her father was a man of the past. The rooks that "caw, cawed" the livelong day in their spring happiness in the tall trees that stretched from east to west behind the old castle, the solemn strike of the old clock, the surly, sullen bell of the tower, the tangled garden, in which creeping plants, fruit-bushes, and blossoms, mingled in a delicious density, out of which arose the old and weather-worn sun-dial, and the cracked fountain,—all the numerous objects of the place, which spoke the undisturbed, the lazy years, were pleasing and daily welcome to the sombered spirit of the new laird. He was not, therefore, for doing more, and his submission to have a band of workmen engaged still further in the work of embellishment, was extorted only for the sake of peace. "Do as you please, then, about these things ; you must leave me my crows and the old clock."

It was evident amid all this activity, by
which many neighbouring sons of toil were set
in motion on good pay, that Miss Mar intended
herself to be a popular person. The peasantry
are everywhere influenced for the better, with
even the appearances of stir and life by which
they are no immediate gainers. A particular
intelligence is often due to their intercourse
with the laird and his friends, and undoubtedly
Morven had for generations owed much in this
respect to the familiarity of the Macalpines.
But for some time they owed little to them in
material interests. The grass-grown avenues,
and the closed windows of the decayed castle, or
mansion, of the local lord, marking his poverty
or his neglect, depress the humble people who
daily look upon the scene, sometimes settling in
their minds a feeling of aversion. Instinctively
they feel that the fairest scenes of their native
land in the possession of him who retains them,
only evidences of his own selfish extravagances
or indifference, outrages one of the highest

social laws ; he is false to the duties of neigh-
bourship as well as to the community.

Now that another reign was establishing
itself, the eyes of many in that district were
brightening up at the work and plenty which
it brought. Miss Mar allowed no breathing
time for the passage of her predecessors ;
instantly setting to work to undo their
memory, by presenting the contrasts of her
own wealth and comfort in no uncertain
appearances. The life and animation of the
place of the Macalpines had gone out with the
stroke which told them that lavishness was no
longer possible. Once upon a time Macalpine
might even have exclaimed with Shenstone,—

> " Of river, valley, mountains, woods and plains,
>   How gladsome once he ranged your native turf ;
>   Your simple scenes how raptured ! ere expense
>   Had lavished thousand ornaments, and taught
>   Convenience to perplex him, art to pall,
>   Pomp to deject, and beauty to displease."

In Miss Mar's estimation, a ruined family's
exit should be an obliteration, and she disliked

to meet, in her survey of the castle or
grounds, a chamber, a wainscot, a tree, a shrub,
an effigy, or a stone cutting, which should
remind her that a woman had been there
before her, who, had she been yet alive,
would have fallen to the lot of obscurity and
poverty ; and she made no secret of her feelings.

Alan forgave the peasantry their seeking
greedily after the new comers. If it pained
him to hear of the obliterations of his family's
mark upon the place, and he resented in his
own mind the indelicate conduct of its new
mistress, he was satisfied that his family's time
had come for renunciation of it,—maintained
too, as it was, to the disadvantage of the
estate itself, and of the people who might benefit from the full operation of its capabilities.
The old laird cursed bitterly all concerned in
these works whenever he could meet with a
listener.

Meantime the county lairds were busily

excited with gossip upon the new addition to their ranks. It appeared, at the first meeting which drew most of these gentlemen together, immediately upon the Colonel's arrival, that Sir Andrew Cameron was the only one who knew anything about him. Only Sir Andrew was disposed to assume the airs of a man intimate with the inhabitants of the world, until he was unmasked. At a subsequent assembly of Commissioners of Supply, one of them uttered sundry ejaculations, potential grunts, which were received as proofs that he knew more of the new-comer than any other. This was Mr Robert Monro, aforesaid, law agent of the Colonel. But Rab was too much the lawyer to divulge a tithe even of the mere physiognomy of his client. Rab was told, as the weeks went on, that his reticent client, who had never yet appeared among his neighbours, was a conscience-stricken man, returned to this country laden with ill-gotten spoils of the natives of India, many of whom had sweated,

if not bled to death, to supply his coffers.
But Rab only gave indignant grunts, and
would reveal nothing.

Sir Andrew Cameron thought himself the
first entitled to wait upon the new proprietor,
and wish him the congratulations of the occasion. It would be seen whether he was to be
visited, or whether he was to remain closed
up with his seared conscience or his diseased
liver. Sir Andrew, too, was nothing loth
to be put forward as a kind of inquisitor.
Wealth was his god, and it was a new pleasure to him to have a near neighbour with
a reputation for riches like Colonel Mar's.
Such was his exquisite sense of the sublime powers of gold, that he never thought
of the alloy.

Sir Andrew had been so far born to the
position he now occupied. He was the nephew
of a greedy laird, representative of a once
powerful clan, and of considerable possessions,
who had clutched every penny of his rents

wherewith to increase his property, and had
driven Andrew from the door, more in angry
ill-will at the poor youth, whose keeping was
solely at the uncle's cost, than in consequence
of the nephew's habit of disobeying the morning call to manual work. The youth, while
showing no quickness of mind in such a situation, and knowing nothing of the purity of a true
Scottish home, was possessed of a dogged energy,
of a kind which never swerved to the right or to
the left from the course set before him ; he
felt bitterly the evils of poverty, and determined on the instant to become rich. Those
who had formerly caressed the heir of the
miserly laird now turned their backs upon him.

The misfortune of beings in his situation is,
that they are sought after only by the mean
and toadyish specimens of their kind, with
whom, upon the removal of the thing they
worshipped, all attention to the individual
vanishes. One alone, in all that country-side,
comforted the friendless youth. Woman,

whose highest mission is her appearance in
the front to the succour of the needy, extended
a temporary asylum. That kindness he re-
quited, he thought, in after years.

The struggle of his life was undeviating in
the design to amass wealth. Having drank
deeply, in all its sour horrors, the cup of de-
pendence nigh to beggary, he knew no remedy
save to live in the object, the want of which
he considered had been the cause of his suffering. He was abroad for many years, and returning with a considerable capital to the
metropolis of the west of Scotland, he attained
the highest position as a merchant. Once in
the possession of a power, he wielded it with
all the surety of a man who has spent more
than a quarter of a century in learning to
attain it ; he rapidly increased his stores, attained magisterial distinction, and received the
honour of knighthood.

Sir Andrew was now, as an elderly man, as
hard as the road he climbed ; he despised the

poor, and was disgusted with the aspect of all suffering; no tender emotion ever suffused his heart; with the pure springs of nature dry and dead, it could not be said truly that he lived for himself, as he did not for others; but he had inherited an excellent digestion, which he had preserved by a moderate life in eating and drinking, and a very moderate conscience in life's troubles. Report at one time said that he had been married in his day; where wife and children were—if they ever existed—was not known. If the subject was hinted at in his presence, it was seen to be painful to him, more so than would have been expected in the case of a man who sneered at the follies, and heart, and other breaks, of his neighbours, as if all human cares were to be set aside.

He was not a shrivelled creature; he talked with a rough energy, which required breadth and lung, putting down every one who stood against him without possessing the force of the physical. He sat now in the drawing-room of Morven Castle, in an immense yellow vest, which had often enough seen service ; his shirt-collar stood erect at one side, and seemed desirous to fall down on the other; but no one would have looked at Sir Andrew twice, to discover from his person, and the material about him, that he was a prosperous man.

Sir Andrew was disappointed with what he saw. He would have liked to have seen the room stuffed with the costly gems and fabrics of the East, whereas he looked upon substantial yet ordinary material.

When the door opened, and in solemn stateliness a lady entered, she banished, so far as she went, the rising feeling of disappointment. If the room was not grand in its way, the cause may have been the artistic design of the lady of the castle, that no splendour should rival that which decked her own person.

Ordinary men saw in Lucretia Mar a very handsome woman, without the tender graces which are expected to accompany the forms of

female beauty. She was not considered fascin-
ating in London society, where she had
recently come out in completeness. Her
manners were stately, almost to heaviness,
and no lustre seemed there to penetrate a
naturally dull complexion, even by the aid of
the dark eye, which certainly looked capable
of fire. She made no response to several at-
tempts at marriage on the part of the men of
the hour who dangle upon the skirts of the
heiress. They bored her, a fact she scarcely
concealed, and she was set down as of sullen
temper. The world has now no time to discover for itself the presence of its heroines,
and it failed to understand her.

Lucretia Mar did not depend upon the
weakly gabblings of male mouths in order to
please her hours. "She was to be stirred by
a man of power," in what direction she did
not exactly know : of course he would be rich,
but beyond that she asked for "assurance of
a man." This had not been given her.

The richest Indian silk enfolded her tall finely chiselled person, and the folds of her dark hair were set with costliest gems; bracelets and rings she wore too, of curious beauty, without altogether attracting the eye from the splendour of the figure, which moved with strong step. Her features were regular enough, forcible, not placid, yet not too pronounced to present harshness. Her face was not remarkable by itself; it did no harm to her. It was full and firm.

A sensitive and refined examiner of her physiognomy might have admired the woman, even upon the discovery of the vulgar element in her character. She was the opposite of insipid, and she was not thought vain. Yet the vulgarity that lay in her came of love of show as well as incapacity for appreciation when not concerned with a will equal or superior to her own. Delicacy, tenderness, and loving sympathy were practically unknown to her. Yet she had sentiment, acquired from

an early and long perusal of the pages of
romance. Her pride was not, certainly, the
consciousness of elevated desires, but her
strength of will, and her conscious power of
using it ; reading fortunately preserved some
form of human love, and she knew how to be
soft and winning.

She knew nothing of Sir Andrew, and, as
she looked upon the old magistrate, a shade
of scorn passed over her face. He saw it not,
but determined to carry away glowing accounts
of her attractions to his nephew.

Sir Andrew introduced himself. It was
not, then, Roderick Macalpine, who, she was
told, might, if the whim seized him, introduce
himself into the castle any day.

"We have been led daily to expect a visit
from the former proprietor," said Miss Mar.

"Very thankful, Miss Mar, you may be if
disappointed," answered the knight.

"He has been unfortunate."

"He is a pest, and a dangerous pest. He

threatened my nephew and heir-presumptive, Captain Hamilton of the Tenth Dragoons, because he presumed, forsooth, to ask of him the price his creditors were asking for the estate. The Captain wished much to call with me now, Miss Mar, but the Earl of Barnton, who is with him, could not be put aside to-day. What a delightful place you are making of the old castle and grounds! We had all need of you, very much need."

" The delight with which these poor wretches of labourers appreciate our work is amusing," she said stiffly.

" You spoil them, Miss Mar. If I might presume to offer you advice, I would counsel you not to spoil them by kindness ; they become good-for-nothing rascals."

The wealthy knight looked pompous. In his later years of prosperity, he spoke of the labourer as of a lower creation to himself. Miss Mar took no pleasure in his advice ; she disliked the knight already.

The times were threatening. The introduction of machinery, a poor harvest, and the disturbance of the financial system, had, at this time, thrown large sections of the hand-to-mouth workers destitute. Fires of homesteads had recently marked the ill-will of the more ignorant peasantry in some parts of England, and Sir Andrew, who knew well the grudge borne against him, dreaded mishap to his own substance.

"We are born in new times, Sir Andrew," the lady said, however. "Once our servants were our men-at-arms, our followers, our protectors, but in these days they are for themselves alone, or become our enemies."

Miss Mar spoke already as if she were descended, at least, from a Norman baron. But the truth was, she was really talking the conventional language to which she had been accustomed.

"It all comes of these d——d wild Frenchmen, who, under pretence of leading the world

to rights, send it back to anarchy. Their
revolutions are the terrors of all right-thinking
men, and are particularly injurious to their
near neighbours like ourselves. I wish we
could transport our island back to the good
old times, which would ever have remained to
us had it not been for these frog-eaters." The
knight laughed loudly.

Men and women forget themselves in the
prosperous gales, and speak the starved instincts
of their situation. Sir Andrew, of course, never
doubted that he would be set down, at any
period of his country's history, with a large
slice of the soil.

The speakers were now joined hastily by
Colonel Mar. He bore about him, more than
on the occasion of his visit to the estate with
the farmer of Finzean, the mark of his Indian
life ; he wore a loose coat of silk, and a scarf of
the same material, and the weather being warm,
his trousers were of bleached linen stuff, contrasting with the dark complexion of his face.

Both Miss Mar and Sir Andrew were in turn surprised when they observed he was evidently caught by them unexpectedly. In the one hand he held a pistol of formidable appearance, and in the other a letter, which he appeared at first to desire to conceal, but on second thoughts held out, as if with the intention of referring to it. His commonly placid eye was excited looking, though his face had something of that over-determined and fixed look it often wore when the weakened frame was conscious of a struggle to meet the call upon it by the stronger spirit.

Colonel Mar apologised for his warlike implement. He had been practising at pistol-shooting, he said, an occupation he was sometimes driven to in the East when banished for long periods from society and literature.

"See, Lucretia," he said, "here is a letter I received in the course of my amusement. It does not concern Sir Andrew, but he may be able to relieve my mind as to the writer of it."

Miss Mar read the letter aloud :—

"MORVEN LODGE, *Monday at noon.*

"SIR,—As I am informed, you have paid a price to certain person or persons for the estate of Morven (where you have taken up your abode), and have, in consideration thereof, received a disposition thereto, with all the usual legal jingle of meiths, marches, &c., I hereby give you notice that said pretended sale is null and void, and of no force and effect whatsoever. I therefore, I, Roderic Macalpine of Morven, hereby desire and require you to remove from the castle and lands, your family, servants, and other cattle. For what damage I have sustained, by your pretended settlement with my pretended creditors, your overturning of the amenity of my policies, your destruction of my works, by which were being perfected some of the most useful inventions of any age, and all in *mala fide*, or at least with reckless haste, and without my knowledge, far less consent, you are held liable to the extent at least of the sum of £100,000, for which an action at law will be immediately instituted against you.—I am, sir,

RODERICK MACALPINE of MORVEN."

Sir Andrew laughed, his portly person heaving between enjoyment of the audacity of the old laird, and delight at the food for gossip with which the incident furnished him.

"This is surely the letter of a madman," said Miss Mar, not much given to laugh at anything.

"It contains no challenge," said Colonel Mar, angry at the noisy knight; "had it done so, I would have regarded my exercise when I received it as rather ominous."

"Colonel," said the daughter, "do not speak that way; to fight with this man, even with paper or speech, must be madness. Send it to your lawyer, if you please; but it is only sound and fury."

"As a magistrate, I must place my *veto* upon Colonel Mar recognising this production as a cause for personal quarrel," said Sir Andrew, bowing to the seriousness he saw demanded of him.

"If this Macalpine is mad, he ought not to be at large, and as a magistrate, Sir Andrew, it is your duty to see to this," answered the Colonel somewhat sternly.

"Faith, Colonel, with that I cannot meddle; there is a method in his madness; he is too old a bird to be caught by the fangs of the law. There is some waggery in this fellow's bursts. I know him of old; he would like to frighten his neighbours who come in his way, but I never knew him succeed in ousting them. It is the law he reckons on, but it's been a broken reed to him all his days, and will not prop him up now."

"Do you think the public opinion of him, as a half-mad person, is such, that the ordinary rule of recognition from one gentleman to another cannot exist in his case?"

Sir Andrew failed to satisfy his host upon the case put to him.

"I hope you are strictly to preserve your game, Colonel Mar," remarked Sir Andrew, who disliked abstractions, to which the Indian was inclined. "Macalpine ruined us all with his carelessness, and you must see you have to make up."

"I have thought nothing of it," answered the Colonel, with some gaiety. "I am not to vex myself to death if I see a rascally son of freedom bagging a hare."

Sir Andrew was puzzled. The Indian was mad.

"My lands are not equal to Morven, and I have five keepers; the neighbourhood was infested with the thieves when I came to it, it's better now; yet such is the state of the people's minds, with these inflammatory talks, that even the schoolmaster, Wat McTavish, is a poacher who escapes the prison with their aid."

"Is not that the name of the man my keeper reports to have seen shoot very early one of

the pheasants I brought with me ? " inquired
Colonel Mar, of his daughter.

It was so.

" The fellow is caught at last, is he ? The
slippery eel is on the hook. He will tremble
in his shoes when he remembers 9 George IV.
chap. lxix., section 13 ; the prison and hard
labour for three months will take the song out
of him. Then, Colonel, have you got him in
your cellar ? "

" In my hall ;—no ! I have done nothing
yet," was the answer.

" Oh, oh ! but leave it to me. I 'll manage
him ; you do not care for the tedious law, and
prefer the easy process of the sword. I 'll have
him at oakum in a twinkle."

Both Colonel Mar and his daughter were
glad to be relieved of the presence of their
neighbour. He was far too fussy and
boisterous for the delicate fibres of the
retired soldier, and his daughter detested the
knight.

To find he had to tranquillise a wounded spirit in the company of Sir Andrew Cameron, was a consummation the Colonel could not face. His daughter found neither the knight, nor the imagination of his nephew and heir-presumptive, relief to her situation.

CHAPTER X.

On the day following the events narrated in the previous chapter, some incidents, trifling in themselves, befell Alan Macalpine, which had an important influence for him. In the morning he met Oliver Arnot, and that respectable farmer had again refused to give him the address of his niece ; moreover, intimating that Ellen herself had distinctly required him to refuse it. We are not always under the influence of our best nature, and Alan went away angry with his old friend, and more particularly with Ellen.

Storms surround the hitches in the progress of love. The self-possessed Juliet exclaimed once of him to whom she was devoted, even unto death—

"Oh that deceit should dwell
In such a gorgeous palace !"

And the hero of this tale of Morven nigh to-day cast off his care for the fair Ellen of Finzean.

Love is not certainly eternal between two beings who have met each other and meandered sweetly on the sunny paths. An eternal bond unites two spirits buffeting bravely the threatening waves around a joint destiny.

A lady in turning a sharp corner on the Morven road at a rapid rate, rode into a drove of cattle. The horse was a high-mettled animal, scarcely for use in these quarters : the rider was herself a tall imposing woman, and, perhaps, required such an animal to make her seat agreeable. It seemed in the act of proceeding, by a wild heave, to throw its rider, when, probably by some accident diverting its attention, luckily it came down upon its four legs, and the services of the gentleman behind the drove were not called on.

The lady was Lucretia Mar and the other Alan Macalpine. She now held her double reins with an assured firmness, in which the two onlookers, Macalpine and his man, saw a more than common strength on the part of the fair rider, while she looked offended at the obstruction on the roadway.

Alan lifted his bonnet, and expressed regret at the danger she had incurred. But she had scarcely deigned to observe him. He was dressed in a light-grey suit, with a broad Highland bonnet on his head, and would have been taken at a glance for a well-to-do farmer. Further observation, however, would at once have detected an ease of bearing, and a refinement and light in his high dark features, which intellectual breeding, combined with strong moral and manly qualities, induce, carrying their possessor out of the narrow mould of any occupation.

Miss Mar's horse still stood, the rider not yet assured ; and she was compelled to return his acknowledgment.

It was no part of her character to be merely ill-tempered, and she asked with sufficient politeness, if there were more cattle following.

Thinking she saw some admiration on the part of a good-looking farmer, she stayed to say a few words more.

"Bucephalus is not accustomed to those shaggy animals," she remarked.

"They are rough-coated and free, like all mountaineers," Alan observed. "Had I known of meeting with this spirited charger, I would have driven them to a side," he continued, still apologetically.

"I doubt if he will ever feel at home here, with these rude roads and passengers," she said.

Loftily she sat and spoke; and Macalpine had experienced a slight sense of resentment, which his sensibility was apt to excite, when her supercilious bearing relaxed, as she looked full in the face of the handsome Highlander who stood erect and proudly at her side.

Miss Mar had ridden out from her castle with the laughing fancy that she could take part in some romantic adventure. She might meet a chief whose only property consisted of blood and claymore, and she would not be sorry to see such a one throw himself at her feet, a loving slave, though she intended never to wed such a man. It was only a trifling beginning to her taste for encounter—this contact with the bright-eyed mountaineer. But she was pleased with it. No woman can look in the face a hero of fancy, however humble in rank, without love, though it live but for a moment.

Alan observed the gleam which stood in the dark complexion of the lady; with easy courtesy, rather than the conventional dignity she would have worn had she gone off at first, she inclined her head and galloped away.

Before Alan rejoined his man, he already believed that the horsewoman was no other than the daughter of Colonel Mar.

"She cannot have known me," said he to himself. "Yet what matters it; she is not a neighbour with whom circumstances permit any intimacy between us." A sensation of pain, which was not weakness, but delicacy, passed through his heart, upon contact with her who had supplanted his own heirship.

"She's a high ane, that!" ejaculated the old drover Donald, as he hit one of his animals idly with the tiny switch which is the badge of the employment of cattle dealing.

"Higher than she should be," remarked Alan, thinking in his dreamy walk only of the beast.

"I was thinking," said Donald, slily, just out of the corner of his mouth, "ye were nae believer in the michty dames."

"Why, you know I prefer the short neck to the long, and the legs not over jointed."

Donald chuckled, and hit away at an animal to hide his delight, but could not help laughing full out.

"She's rin awa wi' yer thochts, short or lang i' the neck, Maister Alan; an' what for no—a fine gay lass wi' as gude a tocher's i' the haill land."

Alan saw his mistake and laughed with Donald.

"Your mind, Donald, seems to run for ever on the fair sex; but you've let the time go without getting your hand tied."

"It's the pat, sir, the pat. I'll be aye thinkin' o' the puir deevils o' Irish fillin' half an acre wi' a dizzen bairns, born to starvation and misery; Lord, Lord, it's a terrible thing to see livin' beings wi' sae little thocht, but it's waur to see them deein' on twa potatoes."

"Richt there," said Alan, who had a keen appreciation of the Scotch humour peculiar to the humbler classes, whose jocularity has generally, at the heart, some moral aphorism. "Yet it's the like of you, Donald, with such opinions, that has deserved the blessings of married life."

"An' deserves them yet," cried the sturdy drover, the only servant of the Macalpines whom it was possible to retain. "I'm as veegorous as I was the year yer father was married, and gin ye haste wi' the new lady o' Morven, odd but I 'll may be hae my lass, Peg Cameron, the same day. I believe i' the Macalpine's auld luck ; they were aye catchin' the young mare when the auld horse fell, and ye 'll just hae yours, like your forbears."

"I am sorry for Peg Cameron," said Alan, "if her happiness depends upon my return to Morven."

The resolution which Alan had made to have no contact with his father's successors at Morven, so far as it could be avoided, he scarcely expected so soon to be called upon to forego. He had not proceeded a mile farther along the road, when Donald espied Mrs McTavish waving a handkerchief as if for them to stop. She was running down the side of a field, which lay between the road where the cattle were being driven and the school-house, and made down upon Alan, out of breath with running and excitement.

Word had been secretly conveyed to Wat that the officers of the law were to be upon him for poaching on Colonel Mar's lands, and he was at present in hiding till he saw what could be done. Alan was the only man Wat and his wife thought of applying to for aid, although remembering he had severely condemned the poacher.

"We've nobody to look to but you, Mister Alan," said the sore-troubled woman. "It's as true as death that Wat was only after specimens"—Wat being also the well known ornithologist of the district—"and this bein' a bit pheasant with a fine colour, he couldna stay his hand. Lord have mercy upon's a' if he's taen up and 'prisoned. I warned him day and night; but he's no guilty of night poaching; would ye but speak to them for my sake and the bairns' sake. There's the

new lady of Morven, she'll no refuse the like
o' you, and bein' but new come cannot be
hard.   O' it's ruin if Wat is taen, he'll lose
the school and beggar himself and all."

Alan was annoyed by what he heard.   He
was angry with the schoolmaster, as he had
always been.

"Ah! you see Wat is all for liberty, as ye
are yourself, Mister Alan, in your own way.
When the farmer comes in grumbling at the
hardship he thinks he must just bear, Wat
takes down a book and a gun and justifies
himself.   He's an impulsive creature, Wat,
and dances into things."

Alan had not intended to refuse his assistance, in so far as he could be of aid, and the
result of Mrs McTavish's entreaties was, that
he was to lay the state of the case before the
proprietor of Morven, and ask him to withdraw
the prosecution, on the understanding that
Wat's gun was to remain in time to come
upon the wall.   He disliked the undertaking,

but he saw Wat himself and believed his story
to be true; he often attributed the reckless-
ness of the class about Morven who poached,
to the licence which his father had even
encouraged, partly, no doubt, because it out-
raged the law which had done so little for
him.

He hastened early to Morven Castle, eager
to get the visit over, by a distaste for the
subject of his advocacy, and for the call at his
old home in the possession of strangers.

As he walked up the already well-trimmed
avenue, the first time since he had left it, in
the evening of this summer day, he asked himself why his step should possess a little dread
and his heart beat less free than it did an
hour before; his emotion was natural, and
he was content to believe that the misfortunes
of his house had not tamed his spirit or excited
it into fury.

But his fancy somehow rested upon Lucretia
Mar. He could not tell how. Yet it seemed

as if some augury had been to point to a link between him and the new mistress of his paternal lands. Morbid, indeed, the fancy, which the rustling of a leaf dispels for ever, he reflected, as he entered the familiar portal.

The ready access to the Master of Morven was not accorded, as of yore ; and Alan waited long in the ante-chamber, and then, when admitted to the presence, it was to that of the mistress.

It appeared to Alan, when he was ushered to the room in which Lucretia Mar reposed after the fatigues of the day, that he was being taken to the presence of some imagined princess. Indian servants preceded him, and a beautiful young female of half colour smiled upon him as he entered, while another sat at the feet of the lady as she reclined upon a couch. The couch was drawn opposite the open window at the head of the room, through which entered, with delicious odour, the air of the summer night, not more than cool, as the sun was only yet declining beneath the hills which stretched their blue and lofty peaks far away to the west.

So far as could be seen—owing to the extensive drapery which enveloped the lady, as a protection apparently from the possibility of chill from the air which came off the mountains—she was in the English attire, and from the upper portion of her dress, it was evidently of the richest and gayest material, and one in which the wearer was pleased to contemplate herself; for upon Lucretia Mar's countenance there often rested the self-complacency which comes of woman's vanity of mere adornment.

Alan Macalpine was not ill-natured, and was not one to cry aloud because a woman showed she was pleased with herself to almost an utter forgetfulness of his presence; but when Lucretia Mar lay still as he reached the head of the room, and scarcely turned her head his way, he was annoyed. He was a philosopher, no doubt; notwithstanding he intended, when another injured him, that other was not to get off scot-free if it were to put down deliberate wrong. There was no more certain feature in the character of the Highlander than that.

What did this woman think? that he was a vulgar and designing intruder, who presumed upon three words spoken in the morning to rush in upon her in the evening? Notwithstanding what she had heard, she now chose to consider that he, who was a farmer and dealer in cattle, must be a very insignificant person, although he appeared to possess some bulk in the eyes of a local gossip like Madge; nay, one to whom the cold shoulder of an affront was necessary, for had not his father written to Colonel Mar a letter the most offensive.

Alan apologised for what he chose to call an intrusion, but he had been ushered in.

Colonel Mar would not be disturbed just at this time; but as she attended as much to affairs as himself, any message might be entrusted to her.

Alan preferred to see Colonel Mar when convenient; he would wait or return again.

Not so, he would better give his message now, or not at all. She felt in Alan's few sentences a cold determination which braced her for a contact; it was not without a certain pleasure to her to treat such a man as she did.

Alan Macalpine had inherited the blood of a race of untamed chieftains of the Scottish wilds, and had never been broken-in to tame subjection. He was boiling with internal rage, which was shown upon his face, first in its intense cold. The snow concealed a volcano. What would have to others been only a disagreeable encounter, was to him a burning at the stake. It was the rankling iron he felt of the world's persecution of prostration.

Slightly, but as apparently happened from the necessity of avoiding the air which blew upon the curtain, Miss Mar glanced by Alan, who had retired a little. She was just able to recognise the hero of her morning adventure. The disdain which she had summoned to her reception of the son of Macalpine prevented any amends. Alan's external, to which almost alone in the first place woman pays her homage, was seen to better advantage than in the fore-noon. His erect form was set off by a suit which became the hour and the visit, and his handsome and romantic cast of countenance told an indignation, which, by the time she saw it, had lit it up with a dignity beyond the brightness and intelligence of its better wear.

Lucretia Mar would not have acted thus had she possessed the refined sensibility of natural woman. Even allowing her vulgar alloy, she must have acted differently had she not been in a capricious humour. She already relented considerably.

" Colonel Mar, sir, is still suffering from his

long continued residence in a warm climate,
and I hope you will not tax him overmuch,"
said his daughter, who now fully revealed the
strength of her frame. Alan had seen at once
that she could not be laid down by illness
since morning.

"I was not aware," answered Alan, "that
Colonel Mar was an invalid, otherwise I would
have addressed him by letter. As it is, it is
not too late to repair my mistake, and I can
take that mode of addressing him."

He turned. Miss Mar did not speak. He
was not yet done.

"Miss Mar probably understands that for
the son of Roderick Macalpine, the present
visit cannot be one of his own seeking. I
come as an intercessor for an erring but
injured man and a helpless wife, who has
pleaded with me to represent facts to Colonel
Mar. I had hoped that Miss Mar was capable
of imagining the unselfishness of my visit—at
all events of setting aside for a moment the

assertion that she was the daughter of the new owner of Morven."

Alan was not one to fly in the fear of his answer, and he paused for an instant. The gaily decked occupant of the couch was struck by an attitude in a gentleman which she had never before experienced. The scorn of the language, rather than the manner of its delivery, excited her resentment—not altogether painful.

"You may interpret, sir, as you please ; I was not prepared to be concerned with any considerations other than my own ; unless it be to give my decision upon the case you may submit to me. I have nothing more to add," haughtily raising herself upon her seat.

"I cannot be expected to rest satisfied with a judge who has admitted such unconcern," replied Alan as haughtily.

"So be it," said Miss Mar, pointing to her servant to ring ; "you will find, on your way, if Colonel Mar can now be seen."

Yet for all this, Macalpine had overcome

Lucretia Mar's distaste to the son of the ruined laird of Morven.

If her character was material loving, it was relieved by her attraction to objects out of the levels. She possessed one of those tempers not too common with her sex, capable of respecting an enemy, and even of being piqued into alliance with one who might gratify her vanity by reciprocating the feeling of an aroused respect. She loved " the unalterable mien" of pride in a man.

" To what do I owe the honour of this visit ?" was the Colonel's short query, before Alan had got beyond the door of the library, in which the Indian was alone with his books. He was standing with one hand leaning on the table at the end nearest the door, while the other was thrust into a scarf which tied the waist of a dressing gown he wore ; he was in that attitude which a gentleman will assume when he is interrupted by an unwel- come visitor.

The Colonel spoke with a startled look, and his frame trembled. He motioned to Alan to sit down, which he himself did. Alan stood, but easily.

"Colonel Mar will understand that I come here simply as a gentleman," said Alan; following his preface quietly with a statement of the case he had taken in hand.

"Do you then disavow the family of Macalpine?" inquired the Colonel sharply as he stared upon Alan; having been able to pay small heed to the tale he told.

"God forbid," was the answer, "that I can ever give offence to my race."

"But you are not proud of them?"

"Proud, as I am entitled to be; proud as most men of ancestry."

"You are descended from Kenneth, the conqueror of the Picts, I understand. That is something."

"The accidents of birth and fortune can give us no title to consideration. I desire to

derive all mine from endeavours to do what is
right."

"You make no claim upon me as a Macalpine?"

"None! My father's name seems in this
house an incitement to anger, and therefore it
was necessary to say at once that my visit has
no connection with self."

"It is a name I would wish to forget,"
Colonel Mar mumbled, and then he sharply
asked if Macalpine had already spoken to his
daughter, making no further inquiry on that
head. He divined, seemingly, something of
what had taken place, wearing for an instant
an expression of anger.

Alan spoke further of his mission, and
pleaded that its success would have a beneficial
effect upon others as well as McTavish.

"You will pardon me some freedom of
speech, perhaps, when I tell you that I was a
friend of your mother." The speaker paused,
while Alan waited as if it were a mystery

being revealed. He never before spoke to one
of the other's rank who particularly claimed that
relation to his dead parent.   "That, however, I
rely upon your honour to repeat to no one.   I
see in you much of her likeness, and something
of that enthusiasm which is the destruction of
our fitness to pursue the course of prudence;
nay, hear me ;. instead of following a pursuit
that leads to the dignity of wealth or fame, I
find you the advocate of poachers and the
preacher up of clowns ; how painful that the
son of my friend could have fallen to this!"

"Risen, perhaps, sir ; I am not the man you
picture ; neither the advocate of poachers nor
the preacher up of clowns ; but the would-be
alleviator of their misfortunes. I pretend to
no enthusiasm beyond the hopes of the future
for the wretched and depressed."

"You have caught the contagion of the
times," said the Colonel, stolidly.

"No, sir, I have not," cried Alan, with fire ;
expressing the emotions of his heart and the

thoughts of his brain regarding the inhuman
and unchristian character of much of modern
life. "I advocate now," he continued, "the
cause of a man whose acts I condemn, but
whose wrong is the return for greater wrong
done by those who sit in places above him.
He was himself taught,—he has bettered the
instruction,—out of rank injustice a thousand
evils live."

"And if I do free this man, what will his
advocate obtain by continuing the redresser of
grievances?" inquired Colonel Mar.

"I will find a reconciliation of this man
with his better nature. I am no advocate of
general clemency, but I will answer in this
case for your kindness yielding the fruit of
reform."

"Recollect my belief, that the fame of a
local demagogue must be dear to you as to
other men," said the owner of Morven, influenced.

"You do not know me," answered the Highlander, with pride, his eyes glistening without painful resentment.

"And you are no more one of us," continued the other.

"Poverty and injustice have taught me to feel the unjust lot of others, without the morbid reflection of what I might have felt, had I been a lord in the Highlands of Scotland," was the answer.

"Well, sir, you speak boldly," replied the other; "but you do not convince me that duty does not call you elsewhere."

"That you may be rid of neighbours whose name you wish to forget," said Alan, with a smile of some humour.

"I am sorry to see you here, where your talent and education cannot be rewarded," remarked Colonel Mar.

"I could have wished," Alan said, "to leave Morven, but my father will not, and I cannot leave him yet. I am making no sacrifice. I acknowledge I am selfish enough to keep my better part to myself. I have no desire to have my heart seared in the market places, nor my soul lost in chasing the illusive honours of fame. I intend to stay where Providence has assigned me the means of a plain and simple, and, I believe withal, a happy life, and an opportunity for doing some fair service."

"You are frank, sir, so am I; I admit I do not desire the residence of Roderick Macalpine so near me, but if I can assist you while I obtain my object with him, I will be doubly pleased. I will place a considerable sum at your service if he and you leave Britain and do not return—at least your father—till I may be no more."

Alan had opened out to the man before him to an extent he little expected. There was a charm about the officer which drew forth a revelation of the enthusiastic portion of himself.

"You do not appreciate the independence I have expressed," Alan answered with sternness,—with scorn it had been altogether, had

he not known the better part of the man he
addressed, and he told Colonel Mar so.

He drew back into himself, sorry in his heart
that he was not altogether understood by a
man with whom he felt some kindred soul
existed.   But he took his departure successful
in his mission.   When he had gone he asked
himself if the offer he had received must indi-
cate a defect in the title of the new proprietor
of Morven.

Not long after Macalpine left the Castle,
Colonel Mar joined his daughter in the drawing-room.   With all her excessive influence
over him, that never went beyond what he
regarded as the lesser things of his life ; in
what lay beyond that he was perfect master,
so much so, that a species of constraint existed
between them, not common to the ordinary
relations of father and daughter.   She had
inherited some caprice from her father, and
his caprice could be worked into slow resolve,
unyielding as the hills.   She sometimes really

believed her position was not positively assured, and she trembled. These were on a few occasions when she dared not have said a contrary word to his wish ; she knew that under the soft manner of these moments he was uttering dire command.

He came into the drawing-room this night, and asked very gently as to what had taken place between Alan Macalpine and her, previous to his call at the library. He sat with her talking pleasantly away for half-an-hour.

In an hour after he left her, Alan Macalpine received and read a letter from her as follows : —" Sir,—I regret that upon your visit here this evening, my preparation to act in an expected disagreeable encounter, to which I was impelled—by evidences not given by yourself, however—led me to carry out my part with injustice. The object of your visit was quite different from that which I was led to expect it to be. I hasten deeply to apologise, and to ask you to excuse what you no

doubt considered unpardonable rudeness, and
to express a hope that what has occurred will
not prevent the growth of those friendly relations in which near neighbours should dwell.
In the sincerity of my regret I place my hope
of your forgiveness for an offence, the excuse
for which you do not likely altogether know.
—Yours truly,   LUCRETIA MAR.".

CHAPTER XI.

WHEN at this time, about midsummer, the first Reform Bill was to become law, after the stormy struggle of the various bodies of the State, the joy was common to the newly enfranchised, and to those who were too poor for the right yet to reach them. The artisan and the peasant, the shopkeeper and the farmer, with one rejoicing welcomed the supposed advent of the reign of plenty. All ranks were penetrated with a sense of power, infusing animation and hope, too commonly exaggerated, but, nevertheless, to bear in time fruit in the enlarged share of " the lower middle class " in the wealth of the country. The proceedings in Parliament had been watched with keen interest by the politicians of Morven. Alan Macalpine had occasionally taken part in the

discussions, actively interested in every movement which bore upon the fortunes of his
country and his fellows. Wat McTavish eagerly
supported Macalpine's views, that much would
needs be done by the individuals themselves,
composing the new constituencies, to procure
a real advantage from the reform. Alan's few
words were listened to with a real interest;
and Wat, anxious to gratify his champion, got
up a requisition on the part of the newly enfranchised and the non-electors, for Alan to
state his views on the subject of the " Franchise
and the People."

There were those, as a matter of course, who
shook their heads at this interference with the
supposed prerogative of the county member,
but the smaller tenants and the cotters signed
to a man; and Alan saw no escape from con-
senting to deliver a lecture in the church, on a
Saturday evening, on the wide subject proposed
to him.

The hour fixed for the lecture was eight in

the evening. At an earlier hour, the same afternoon, there were arrivals at Morven Castle to partake of a feast which had been provided by Colonel Mar. His daughter had yearned ever since her coming to make a display to such of the people of the county as she could well invite. The Tory faction, composed of nearly all the landowners of the county, was too strong to put itself to the trouble of doing particular suavity to the new proprietor of Morven. Those of them who affected the highest society of the Capitals, doubted Colonel Mar and his daughter; and there had been refusals to attend this dinner party. Yet, the announcement was no sooner made by Sir Andrew Cameron, that the new laird was of the right colour, than several members of the party were ready to partake of his hospitality; and there were not wanting sons in the county families quite equal to appreciating a marital interest in the rents of the barony of Morven. Sir Andrew Cameron's nephew, Captain Hamil-

ton, was one of these—a young officer of some
twenty-six summers—whose most intense feeling was disgust that his uncle had been
connected with trade, although he was himself
the son of a man who had been found incapable
of earning his bread by trade, and had become
a small official of the excise. The son had
inherited some of the doggedness of the
Camerons; and Sir Andrew thought he was
not, altogether, without credit in his choice of
an heir. The laird of Glenballoch, his wife,
and eldest son, regarded themselves as the
chief guests of the feast; they looked and
acted the "oldest family" in the county. The
family had never increased its possessions;
and without admitting the fact to each other,
or to themselves, one and all had half-grown
convictions, that in these times it was desirable
the estates should be enlarged.

Grant of Ballatruim—invariably referred
and spoken to as Ballatruim—was not behind
with his sense of his personal or family im-

portance; his paternal miles exceeded those of Glenballoch, and his ambition was to be the leading man of the county. In this he was certain to fail; he possessed neither the forces of ability nor the supports of pride; vanity inflated him.

Ogilvie of Stronach was of another stamp —gay, volatile, and dissipated, but highly educated, and reasonably facetious in political feeling, when not under excitement. If he were unscrupulous, it was not out of calculation based on hard selfishness; he was regardless of consequences, because his humour happened, for the time, to have been crossed, and he was not, therefore, particular as to the character of the pursuit, provided it admitted of diversion.

Besides Robert Munro, the writer, from Morven, there was the clergyman of the parish, a pastor who had married, upon one hundred and fifty pounds a year, a woman with scanty ideas, but with activity, in all respects, towards the full provision of food and clothing;

and the Rev. Malcolm Alexander soon became too interested in pork-curing and beer-brewing, to admit of any real abstracted existence upon the life within. The sheriff and two officers from the county town, and an extensive brewer and his wife from Edinburgh, tenants on the estate, who happened to be then in the neighbourhood, completed the list of guests at Morven Castle.

It was the old story for Lucretia Mar. Her guests had scarcely met, when she desired them gone. She felt the presence of a weary assembly; while she chid herself for permitting the feeling, with a consciousness that she was too indolent to animate the party.

Colonel Mar discussed with the Glenballoch family, the weather, and the difference between the climate of Britain and that of India. Sir Andrew Cameron reckoned with the brewer the extent of the fortunes now being realised here and there in commerce, while his nephew, the captain, at the other end of the table,

stigmatised trade as the ruin of the native
glory of Britain, and in reality, by its engross-
ing power, the forerunner of her degeneracy
in the race of nations. Ballatruim sympa-
thised with the king in his recent dilemma as
respects reform. The officers discussed sporting prospects, though there was not much
prospect for any of them doing destruction in
the forthcoming season on the moors. In
short, the company thrashed the straw which
alone formed the provender of the conversation. Ogilvie, in the presence of the ladies,
hazarded sallies of his humour without making
any impression upon the dull mass of life that
had assembled for enjoyment. The hostess
alone seemed willing to applaud the attempt,
and, if really feeling mirthful, might have
awakened those of the assembly in whom the
sense of nature's early sweets was not altogether extinguished. But after Glenballoch
had in a few pompous phrases toasted Colonel
Mar, the ladies rose. Ogilvie determined that

there should, if possible, be some variety in the
talk, if it were only to amuse himself.

"Why, you know, gentlemen, I'm as staunch
a Tory as lives in the county, but I think we
have deserved this beating on the reform question," he said, with an air of frankness.

"Deserved, sir! how deserved?" inquired
Glenballoch, angrily.

"We have waited," answered Ogilvie, "till
the broom has been set in motion to sweep all
away, whereas, had we ourselves done a moderate brush at the cobwebs, and burnished the
old fixtures, nothing more would have been
required."

"Ah!" answered Glenballoch, aroused by
the seeming imputation on the worth of his
class, "let sleeping dogs lie, they'll bite the
more if they find they are awakened to be
deceived with a dry bone."

"Now," said Ballatruim; he generally began
with an emphatic "now," as indicating that
the judgment of the case was reached in what

he had to say; "I regard the present times
as lost to any true sense of loyalty and honour.
I have studied the history of nations from the
days of Homer, and see to the bottom of the
mind of every thinker on political science
worthy of the name, and my opinion is, that
nations who lose their one common heart of
devotion to their monarch become impoverished
and fall into decay. I am descended from a
Jacobite race, and I am prouder of that, sir,
than I am of my miles, for we cannot say acres
here, Colonel, as you perceive."

"Come, Ballatruim," broke in Ogilvie, "your
father was a favourite with the villagers, Whigs
to a man, and might have solicited their suf-
frages had he lived."

"No, sir," answered the other, indignant at
what he saw was meant neither altogether in
jest nor in earnest; "my father was above
attraction for the rabble."

"Yet," said Ogilvie, "it is generally reported
that you—yourself, quite lately, were seen in

the most friendly conversation with young Macalpine."

" He who is talking sedition, or something worse in the parish church ? " ejaculated the brewer.

" How comes this ? " asked Glenballoch, angrily.

Colonel Mar came to the rescue.

" I agree with Ballatruim," he said, " that the king has been shamefully used by the mob. I am for an absolute monarch, if he is a true man, who will preserve the nation from anarchy. Our king must please all, and he pleases none ; he must sympathise with all, and yet have no positive mind of his own, and so becomes a powerless puppet."

Toasts now became general, and the Colonel who had several months led a half solitary life, wakened up and became excited. He told tales of Indian life ; now laughed, and then became sad. He was rich with memories pleasing to most present; there were those yet untold under which he writhed, did he approach the thought of thinking of them.

"I have served my country, and I have served myself," said the host, whom wine made very open and communicative. "You talk of political principles as if they were religion: no man can deny that he thinks as he believes he will serve himself best. Yes, in religion the very faith we profess is sugared to our swallowing by holding out the return of a saved soul."

This was treading upon ground none present had ever cared to enter upon. There was a mockery in the speaker's heart,—mockery of his own life, of the guests sitting at his table.

The Colonel proceeded—

"Once upon a time I was all loyalty. I did not consider myself in the first instance,—the king—my friend—woman—that frail thing who brought sin into the world, were the objects of my unselfish loyalty. But I awoke to the falsity of my devotion; all the incense

I had offered up was unappreciated as the gusts on the housetops. I was passed over in the service I had chosen, where merit was my only passport to favour ; my friend passed me by in time as one incapable of rising in the world, and therefore of serving him ; and the woman I loved with intense and disinterested passion, threw it aside to embrace—a villain. Can you be surprised then, gentlemen, that my course of life changed. I sought wealth, and I have found it. That, at all events, is real. India has been my salvation from the world's contumely, and I have been revenged. But one thing requires to be done, one terrible bond to be redeemed—one man to be shot," here the speaker's eyes, which had spoken with a brilliancy enthralling to his guests, suddenly became glassy, as if the working of an over-charged brain had been too much for the delicate frame of the speaker.

In an instant, and by violent effort, which showed the self-command, over even his weak frame, he was capable of exercising, Colonel Mar recovered himself. The warm climate, he said, had affected his brain and nerves, and he was apt to wander in his speech upon any excitement, but the illness was only moment-ary: a glass of cold water relieved him.

The evening went on with Colonel Mar as before; as to his guests, all believed their host to be a conscience-stricken man, who had involuntarily revealed the crime of his Indian life. Glenballoch especially inwardly cursed his coming to the dwelling of such a man, and except in the cases of the lawyer, Ogilvie, Sir Andrew Cameron, and Captain Hamilton, the wine which the party drank and highly praised soured within them, by the horrible imagina-tion that it had been set upon the table be-fore them purchased by the blood of man. All the tales of Eastern cruelty and murder with which the popular mind connected the splendour of the rich nabob entered into their minds.

" I wonder," inquired the youngest military man present, desirous to turn the conversation, " whether discussion is allowed at the church to-night ? " It simply occurred to the ingenuous youth that he might gain favour by a proposal which might break up the party quickly, and he suggested that an attempt should be made to challenge any democratic opinions.

" That 's a subject I was about to introduce," said Ogilvie. " We do not support our principles by public advocacy, as if we believed in them, while the radical's heart is in his mouth. Here is young Macalpine carrying all before him."

Colonel Mar at once placed his pew at the service of whomever cared to go.

It was now Ballatruim's turn to exhibit the effect upon a weak brain of wine, and of the joint stimulus of passion. He had been wounded and badgered by the one suggestion of desertion from the family principles, just as

such a person can be by a free and careless
fellow like Ogilvie, with enough good nature
in his character to prevent the rage falling
upon himself. Ballatruim was angry with himself, with his landlord, and with the rest of
the guests. He was enraged against Alan
Macalpine, whose slight connection with him
was giving cause to casting stains upon his
honour.

"I care not for any man's aspersions," said
Ballatruim, "so long as my own conscience is
clear. But I can show you how active are my
principles." So saying he walked out of the
room, flushed with wine and rage. He looked
hard upon the ground, endeavouring without
success to clear his brain of the fumes which
obscured their not ordinarily too great brightness. Meanwhile the others desired to escape
from that feeling of oppression which Colonel
Mar's words of blood had caused. Carriages
were called, and the ladies joined their hus-
bands in hurrying away, learning very soon

that there was something wrong. Ogilvie was all activity to secure a party for the meeting at the church, which consisted by his exertions, besides Ballatruim, of Captain Hamilton, three of the officers, and Miss Mar, who appeared not averse to any adventure such as the visit seemed to promise.

CHAPTER XII.

As the minute hand of the old village clock turned the half hour after seven o'clock on the Saturday evening aforesaid, there was something more than common in the movements of the Morven people. The usual knots of Saturday evening loiterers were in greater numbers, and spoke louder; the keepers of the few shops were at their doors instead of at the counters, where the "change" usually was brisk at this time of that day; the carts of the small farmers still stood in the village square unyoked, to the delight of the urchins, while their owners refreshed fuller than usual at the tap-room of the inn. There never had been an assembly such as this in Morven, and the inhabitants of the place were fully sensible of its importance.

Many walked towards the church with an
elasticity they had not before known, born of
an idea that somehow there was a new vital
hope arisen for them ; though in some the aspiration was somewhat obscured because they
did not see at once its practical realisation.
Conspicuous was a band of the chief or managing
servants, ploughmen, and shepherds of the
farms on the Morven estate, and one or two
others of the eastern district.

The Morven people had, since the coming of
Alan's mother, been housed, fed, clothed, and
even educated better than was commonly the
case in the county ; these were in truth as excellent specimens as might be seen anywhere
of the hardy and independent Scot. Morven
is not in the remote Highlands, but stretches
to the Lowland line, where it is remarked the
broadest and purest Scotch is spoken. The
Morveners were not generally Highlanders pure
and simple ; looking rather the descendants of
that national race which had secured by their

often solitary support of Wallace and Bruce
the freedom of their native land, than the sons
of the mountain, bound to local tradition, their
own fastnesses, and the chiefs that led them.
Their well knit frames, and fair and prominent
features, upon which was the hue of perfect
health, spoke the generous vigour of their individual lives, and of their national history.

These, however, formed rather the cream
than the bulk. A fearful degeneracy was
visible in many who came from the higher
parts above Morven, where, it would be found,
they had met with harshness or neglect. Of the
better class of whom we have spoken Alan
Macalpine was proud. Rude only in the sense
of being natural, beneath lay a deep acquaintance with the Bible and a literature of poetry and
history, whose influence upon their emotions
and conduct was worth more than the study of
half the classic pages or learned tomes of the
world. Their music is as stirring and plaintive
as their song—direct to the heart these go.

While Jamie's soul warmed at his energetic delivery of "Scots wha ha'e wi' Wallace bled," or
the Jacobite Colin saddened with "Bonnie Char-
lie's noo awa'," Jean, as she parted with her
"Brandy" and "Blackie" cows for the night,
heard her charms acknowledged as the bonnie
lassie of "The Kye comes hame" by some more
domesticated swain ; she being able herself
slily to return the compliment, through her
long acquaintance with the well thumbed
"Burns." Among these, by natural solidity of
mind, and gentleness of humour, were the
equals of man whom wealth and rank had
greatly influenced to the forgetfulness of nature.

"The great body of the agriculturists in the
service of others are foully lodged, fed, taught,
and recreated," Alan reflected, intending that
his lecture should be much for their benefit.
"A sense of justice on the part of the owners
of the soil, and an expenditure by no means
large, might give the tillers of the ground, and
the tenders of sheep and oxen, a chance to

reach their due place in the national life.
They may become a power in influencing
society and strengthening the nation ; they are
at present dead as the unheeded rush-roots of
the winter stream—often dead to themselves,
generally dead to others. Society should be
elevated and recreated by the infusion of life
from below and from above. The ranks are
repellent by the misery and ignorance of the
one, and the exclusiveness and ignorance of the
other. Not kindness but sympathy has been
said to be needful to bind the bursting bonds
which ought to unite the classes of the land.
This must grow to fellowship ; without that
there will be no real sympathy. Men must
meet as equals all round irrespective of their
rank or wealth ; all must conspire to the
general elevation. Meantime the cultured
must seek to find food for fellowship. The
Lord of men, who thought it no robbery to
be equal with God, drew Himself to the company of publicans and sinners. He could

penetrate the masks of life, and find interest
there as well as a noble purpose. Has Christianity followed Him after this free, human,
way of elevating others ? "

Alan went into the precentor's desk amid
the awkward applause of a country audience
quite unaccustomed to such manifestations.
The schoolmaster was briskly about, seeming to
be everywhere present at the same time. The
beaming countenance of Oliver Arnot frowned
a little as Wat came upon him, but he was
unable to withstand the frank address of the
now reformed poacher. Arnot was late, and
Alan could not conceal a smile as he observed
the scene being enacted between the two. He
knew that so decided a Tory came there from
the promptings of a hearty spirit towards himself.

After the lecturer had been seated, one of
the audience was seen to rise, evidently intending to speak. There were no cries of "Sit
down," and "Put him out," as would have

rushed from the throats of a town assembly,
and the man stared about him with a face
expressive of bewilderment, fear, and wretched-
ness. McTavish rose, but Alan motioned him
to let the man alone. He still stood as if the
words he had intended to utter had vanished
from his tongue, or his heart was too full of
suffering to permit his physical powers their
free use. He sat among the crofters of Sir
Andrew Cameron's estate, who were together
apart, having resolved to come at the last
hour. Poor souls, they were hanging between
the life and death of their whole world here,
and grasped the invitation of the young politician as weary drowning men seize the straw
blown by the wind. Most had the look of
men who were depressed and worn out with
poverty and care : many were thin, bent, and
rheumatic ; the blood stood in the corners of
their little flesh, though their anxious yet
dimmed eyes indicated that suffering still provided them with forces of reflection.

Alan inquired gently of the old man if he desired to speak. The slowness, he knew, came of decay, and he was content to wait as the crofter wiped with his tattered rag the sweat which had gathered on his forehead.

" It 's Elshie," cried a dozen voices near by him.

" I have that to say that maun be said," said the old man with a great effort, "and that before ye begin, sir. I have lived on the Cameron estate, laddie and man, above half a century, and now I maun quit it wi' the rest o' them. Man, woman, and bairn have been warned to quit if they come here this nicht— and we 're here." The man's voice went from him as he thought of their separation from their old home and the terrors of such a change. He sat down ; he could say no more ; his feelings had overmastered him. He muttered, in the silence of the sympathy which was felt for him, " We glory in being here ;

and Andrew Cameron will have the deil on his neck some day."

The careworn face assumed a look of pride as he spoke his emotion in these few words. Alan looked into the dimmed eyes of the stricken man, and read a soul which had risen in these few moments far beyond comparison with the man's who had done him the wrong. It was his first and his last thrust at a mean world which had robbed him of his happiness.

Whispers of commiseration went through the church, and all turned to the lecturer to observe how he would treat this interference with liberty. Alan's heart was deeply affected, and his spirit burned with indignation. It was his first practical lesson in the vicious courses of some politicians. He said he had not believed that such tyranny now existed; the tale made him shudder as he had done on reading the black pages of history. He would have advised the crofters not to come, had he known of the threat. Meantime he would proceed with the lecture, and they would consider at the close what should be done.

The lecturer began by an explanation of how he came to address them, and then sprung with enthusiastic leap into his subject, which rather appertained to social progress than politics proper. The practical solution of the difficulty in elevating the masses to their due life, he left to another occasion. The abolition of the Entail Law, of the law of Primogeniture, and various other questions, he left alone. His object, then, was to show that the wellbeing of all was the wellbeing of each, and that the progress of the people and the national strength would be chiefly promoted by true appreciation of their moral and intellectual being. He relished political discussion only as it tended to the promotion of individual happiness and the national strength ; and he uttered his views not only for the hearing of those present, but for those elsewhere interested.

Too high expectations had been formed in the minds of the people as to what the possession of the franchise by itself could do for them. It was an engine of power, but would confer no benefit upon them without exercising all those qualities of mind and body necessary to the due use and guidance of the machinery. He demanded thought, and a seeking after greater knowledge of moral and physical science, which even the most simply educated could largely command by his own exertion. Rank, wealth, and the culture the people did not possess, would hold the sovereignty in the nation, until the mass reached a higher standard in knowledge and right aspiration. Wealth and rank distributed immense influence of all kinds upon the mass, which gave none in return except its call for more power; while his ambition was to see a community entirely great, and having a vast influence,

without any consideration whatever of such
elements as these. The mass had now rather
to seek the advantages by which the power
they already possessed could be made effec-
tual—knowledge, and equal privileges in the
application of it. To that end all their efforts
must be directed, not for the purpose of finding greater power as an end and for selfish
gratification, but as a means of raising the
mass of happiness through moral worth, security, independence, and national strength.
The frantic acts of blood-heated men would
never better the condition of themselves or
their country; they must act, but with the
lever power of well-grounded beliefs and aspirations. An intense sense of personal injustice, however unlearned, might command
redress; but limited in its appreciation, it sank
with the effort. There must be a sensitive
understanding seeking after the national welfare, before the design of any individual in
political movement could be true. Upon rank

and accumulated material wealth men had been accustomed to look with occupied eyes, so that they came to regard these as the enduring elements of strength, creating an incapacity for the truer riches of man's own being : the husks were fast coming to take the place which should be occupied by the kernel, so powerful were the externals of the world upon men's minds. This material sense must largely fade with all men before a real progress could be made, when nature, in the simplicity and grandeur of its power, will have a true operation. To the common brotherhood we hastened only when a sense of this truth leapt in the veins. A vast revolution was required to a great extent in men's minds. With this vein of belief in nature, as opposed to the show of the world, arises a sense of living not alone for ourselves but also for others. " Seek not thine own, but each another's wealth," says St Paul ; and Christianity, which founds its common life upon the simplicity of nature, is alto-

gether despised when not attended to in this
living spirit of brotherhood. By the glowing
thoughts of heaven, or the terrors of hell, man
must be aroused to this as the first need of his
daily action. As it grew, fully but moderately
always, and with no senseless lavishness, men
would reap the harvest by a toil which would
not necessitate the one extreme of a debasing
or destroying scramble for bare existence, or
permit the other of an inglorious and prodigal
ease. With this spirit would exist industry,
but no ambition to amass,—temperance and
no repletion,—each individual living with
the proud possession of a noble law which he
fulfilled in the commonest concerns. " The
starving wretch who steals a piece of bread,"
said the lecturer, " is execrated by a society
which sees nothing to blush at in prodigalities;
yet the latter are most criminal, which debase
not only the offender himself, but defraud
many others through the law which enables
him to deal with what he holds without any

account." Each who would not perish, but
live, had an equal liberty to the bringing of
an era of a higher and more active sense of
duty. How glorious a crown—unknown as it
might be to the world—gained in such a cause,
compared with the baubles which fall to the
votary of mere common personal ambition!
But how was it in the world? Life was still
the banquet of the philosopher, from which we
must prepare to quit to give place to others.
But was the presence of the Master of the
Feast acknowledged or ignored? " Would to
God," cried the lecturer, " He were not generally ignored. The Creator has provided
unlimited sources of happiness for our just
appetites, and we cut each other's throats, tear
out each other's eyes, and scramble for the
provision at the table with the ravenous and
malicious mouths of wolves ; we wrangle and
push the others from their stools, and look
upon men who are brothers as antagonists,
to be destroyed or subjected to isolation and

fall." To those whose lives were much a struggle to keep existence together, the appeal to seek other considerations was altogether vain.

> " Chill penury repressed their noble rage,
> And froze the genial current of their soul."

Bitter grief and rage rested for ever in his heart that such a condition of things existed in a Christian land of plenty. In his own experience the sight was but little owing to the sufferers themselves. The utter selfishness of men was largely the cause of it. " Let each man here," said the lecturer, " resolve to do what in him lies to remedy so cruel a sin. By his sympathy and labour for the fallen he will conciliate the hand of heaven, which prepares its avenging bolts for the perpetrators and indifferent seers of iniquity."

The lecturer then proceeded with some history of divisions in the life of nations, and usurpation of sections, by which came their downfall. Greece, Rome, modern Poland, and

France, illustrated this subject: that where life beat only in a part of the body it must die. The history of Poland gave a painful example of brave and heroic gentlemen endeavouring to sustain a nation, at the bottom of which lay repressed masses. France was a body continually rife with matter for the political analyst. France would have been saved the horrors of her fevers if the peasantry had not been, previous to the great Revolution, trodden under foot of the landed magnates; and while the towns were permitted to breed in squalid dens hordes of men and women who were so far left to their misery as to find passion's sway in the frenzies of revolution, the nation became a victim to its own crime, and the cause of humanity was wounded to the quick. He disliked large towns as a man and as a politician—they engendered disease of body and mind; yet there was nothing done to retain men in the country; the whole movement of the times was rather to drive them from it. Short-sighted as well as cruel policy! Prussia had taken warning from France; aroused out of her sleep in the misfortunes which befell her in the wars of Napoleon, she had hastened to call into life the strength of the nation. The king at his own hand abolished the seigneurial prerogatives of the feudal gentry; he granted constitutions to the towns and burghs, and decreed the essentially democratic institutions of compulsory education and the landwehr, a system of military service in which there was an absence of privilege and a disregard of rank and wealth. Prussia will reap the harvest she has sown. She will boast of having among her children neither mere idlers of fashion nor miserable rascals; neither those who gather to labour only as elements of dispeace, nor useless consumers of others' labours. Her people increase in moral and intellectual vigour. The nation becomes invincible on its own soil.

Macalpine now particularly addressed himself to those present. It was natural for him, he said, to bestow the greatest share of his affectionate regard upon the rural people or peasantry. "The peasantry of our land," he said, "have been in ancient times strong as free. They have degenerated in importance. It was they who, being deserted by the nobles in the times when Scotland was threatened with national extinction, rallied around the standard of the hero, and fought out her independence with their blood. To them we owe greatly the freedom and spirit of our native land ; and that should be for ever remembered, that the peasantry may be restored to a just strength commensurate with the growth of the nation ; promoting thus, too, an increase of the national strength and glory. Woe be to those and their time who commit aught by which the brave sons of the soil degenerate and fall away from their better selves, rather than increase in numbers and vigour. Upon them I will lay much of any misfortune—let us hope

only peril—which befalls our native land.
Wealth and talent, and an intelligent town-
bred population, we have got ; but without the
proud sons of the mountain and the strath,
still glowing with the fire of their fathers, and
love of their fathers' and their own homes, the
land may become an assortment of moving
mummies, readily falling a prey to its
enemies."

Farmers were called upon to bestir themselves, to aid in the improvement of the soil,
by which larger supplies of food would be
obtained ; labourers were bound to call for a
thorough advance in the comforts and recrea-
tions of life. He came, then, to speak of those
who suffered degeneracy, keeping no pace with
the material progress of the age, and falling
far behind their due place in the corporate
society—the body of peasants or small farmers,
or crofters and general labourers on the soil.
Why should they at that time be often huddled
in hovels rather than in sweet and convenient

cottages ? why should they trudge on in daily
unremitting labour without fair hopes of
advance in things needful to promote and
keep up the charm of existence ? Religion
and morals stood paramount, but man could
not live by these ; his imagination dulled, he
could but dimly perceive that greatness
attained by living in them. The envy of the
jaded man of pleasure, or of him with sordid
and vain passions, could never be aroused at
the sight of dull or meagre content. He
wished the strong, free, and joyous peasant
to fulfil a picture of true happiness to the
world. That picture was not often there,
surrounded as its material was by the sublime
and the beautiful in nature ; human life in its
midst was neither sufficiently attended to in
material needs and in education—and therefore most often desecrated—to permit of the
charm being continued to it. Sad story ! And
it was frequently cast out in consequence. It
was the duty of every patriot to hasten the

time when this would be no longer so. The
happiness of the whole people, the national
strength, was concerned in the work of restor-
ing to the soil, men in a condition vigorous on
all sides. He said that the colonial policy,
stigmatised by Brougham as "allotting the
sweat and dust to the African, and securing
to the European the fruit and the shade," was
really the policy of some Britons towards their
own countrymen, who were retained in a vir-
tual subjection, or driven off the face of the
land. The land of the crofter had largely
become, and was becoming still, the desolate
sheep range and the deer forest. The land
that God designed for the nurture of the
hardiest race of men, was given over to the
beast and the occasional tread of the man of
purse. What were even some so-called im-
provements to those who had associated with
the scenes the completeness of their days?
There were other rights as just as the rights
of property. Property must be treated so as

to give access to its fullest benefits for the general weal. The nation was entitled to see that property was justly used for the communal benefit. It must be managed with a due regard to the welfare of the immediate community and the nation at large.

Too learned and aspiring for their daily lives the audience generally considered the lecture to be, though they were none the less pleased; the enthusiastic manner of the speaker fully showing his own belief in the justice and realisation of his picture. There was loud applause by the stamping of heavy feet and cries of " bravo," and " hurrah," as Alan uttered the closing word.

The party from Morven Castle entered the church and took possession of the Colonel's pew, just as Alan was entering upon his sympathetic description of the Polish nationality. Their appearance occasioned much surprise, and also some interruption.

Ballatruim's entrance had caused particular

wonder; but it was whispered he was the
worse of his wine. He sat with his hands
joined before him supporting his irresolute
looking mouth. He stared hard at the
lecturer, and two or three times gave a
querulous grunt which drew all eyes upon
him, and latterly the cold, determined look of
Macalpine. He was abashed only as an
inflamed man is who postpones evil inten-
tions. Captain Hamilton and others who
were cool enough fully to comprehend what
they heard were boiling with rage, while too
much alive to some recent events to hazard
decided interruption.

There was one occupant of the pew who
listened with very different feelings from the
others. This was Lucretia Mar. She was not
a Tory; the party had no attraction for her
restless spirit. She hated the past as she
knew it, and as she believed the Tory rejoiced
altogether in it, she disliked Toryism. Stag-
nation she detested; and it seemed to her that

her life had grown up in a state little better. Always had been dinned into her ears the old worn platitudes of party, until "political principles" became to her one dull unmusical monotone, reserved for old men to harp at for want of energy to enunciate a deep harmony out of the broad, many-keyed instrument, humanity. It seemed to her that if Macalpine were a specimen of the Radical, these men were not what they had always been represented. She had learned to think of them as political murderers, who plotted the death of the State. She was now carried away by the enthusiastic heart which sent forth flashes in the enunciated and yet calm tones of his well modulated voice ; the, to her, singularly ideal and aspiring fervour of his sentiment charmed her. There was a power in the speaker she had not heretofore witnessed, and she was captivated by it, not as an inflammable girl, but as a woman of the world, with a temper to some extent above

woman's commoner vanities, embraces the
realisation of some vision of man loftier and
stronger than those she is accustomed with at
her side.

That night she had been struck to the quick
at the cold leave-taking, particularly of the
ladies of her party.   She was quick at reading
others, and she felt they intimated a desire not
to see her again.   She cared not, nor was hurt ;
she despised, and to-night she was drawn towards
the denouncer of, stiff " people of privilege."

" Now," said Alan, " that I have laid down
my paper, I would return to the subject we were
called on to attend to before I began."   It was
evident he was now done with any ideality
with which he may have excited his mind in
the closet.   He was in the presence of the
actual.   The antagonistic growls of Ballatruim
and some of the other occupants of the Morven
pew, had irritated the spirit of indignation
excited within him by the tyrannic conduct
of Sir Andrew Cameron.

"No," cried Ballatruim, rising instantly upon his legs, flushed and unsteady ; "you are a rebel, and have spread sedition in this church, for which you must answer."

"That may be your opinion, sir," was Macalpine's calm but firm reply. "This meeting was not called for discussion, though," he added ; "should you desire to defend your opinions, I doubt not my audience will listen to you."

Alan sat down as if to hear the laird further.

"I am not here to bandy words with such people," said Ballatruim, furious at the other's coolness. "I am a magistrate, and I forbid this meeting proceeding further."

This speech caused a titter even among the company in the Morven pew. It was delivered with all Ballatruim's dignity, but was late by nearly half a century.

"Since discussion then is not to be attempted," Alan went on with calm dignity,

"I ask that this meeting pass a resolution regarding the crofters who have been threatened with removal for attending. I characterize the threat as tyrannical, and view it with indignation and shame; and move that it be so set down in writing, and the minute forwarded to every landlord in the county."

"I will burn it unopened, and thrash the beggarly hound who brings it," cried Ballatruim.

"This is no case for begging. The authors of such cowardly practices must be overwhelmed with public opprobrium," answered the lecturer, still calm.

"Do you mean me? I demand to know if I am included," cried Ballatruim.

Alan was determined not to allow his temper to give way at this repeated provocation, yet it was an abuse of Ballatruim's authority which wounded his pride. He rose again, and, addressing Ballatruim, said, "I demand that you sit down, and cease to interrupt, otherwise it will be necessary to expel you from the church."

Some of the agriculturists, unused to see the laird's authority questioned in the least degree, quivered at the language of their champion.

Ballatruim, with the demon of revenge in his heart, silently prepared himself to inflict a blow which should startle his enemy with its completeness and suddenness. Groping with one of his long arms, he took hold of a small footstool which he found opportunely at the feet of Lucretia Mar, who sat on his right hand. Gently he drew it up on his knee.

Meanwhile, Oliver Arnot seconded the motion which had just been made. He said he was a Tory of the old school, who would never see a good neighbour starve so long as he had a loaf and a can of milk to share with him. He was no man for changes, but he was horrified to hear the story of Elshie, and he seconded the motion of Mr Alan Macalpine.

"And now for a vote of thanks," were the words of McTavish, jauntily, ere he had yet time to rise from his seat.

"There!" howled a voice which resounded in the small church. All eyes were turned towards Ballatruim, and there, overhead, he grasped with the full grip of his right hand the edge of the stool, while one of the legs was in the left hand of Miss Mar, who held it so tight that her arm was strained in the effort. Caught, as he was, by the watchful and quick energy of a woman, the force of the iniquity he purposed struck him with shame, and he sank upon the seat like a helpless drunkard. The incident was the signal for great commotion. The door of the church had been for some time partially ajar, through which, now and again, little crowds of farm servants and the less intelligent of the villagers, endeavoured to listen, without incurring the dangers to place and employment they believed consequent upon their full countenance of the meet-

ing. Among these were conspicuous several
servants of Ballatruim and of Sir Andrew
Cameron. These, observing something of what
was going on, opened the door full wide, just
as some labourers and others in the pews beside the Morven one rose as if to hold the
savage Ballatruim. Imagining this was the
signal for attack upon the laird, a cry arose
from without that he was being murdered,
which in the agitation of the times spread far
and fast. Armed with sticks, these burst in
in a seething mass, and the audience near the
door were driven forward into the body of the
church. The frail wood-work of the pews
beside the Morven one gave way, and the
men in possession of Ballatruim were, with the
loud and coarse curse of an infuriated band,
struck heavily by their assailants.

In the general commotion, the endeavours
of Alan and others to command attention
were unheard. No man seemed to comprehend whence this sudden fury had arisen, and

the deepening darkness lent a mystery to it, as it seemed expended in no rational endeavour, but only to strike down those nearest to hand, whether friend or foe.

The western door was now thrown open, and many made their way towards it, including the occupants of the Morven pew, with the exception of Ballatruim, who was in the hold of half-a-dozen men. Alan had not left his seat, prominent though it was for any missile, and the pulpit and steps were occupied by a band of his supporters who, in their loud cries for order, added to the confusion. Miss Mar, yet unhurt, stood fearful of the crush in front of the desk. The danger was at her side, for the insensate crowd was pressing onward, and she might be trampled down or smothered. By a clever leap, Alan reached and seized hold of her, and with some pain to himself, half lifted her into the desk — she was safe.

"I have scarcely deserved this," she whis-

pered to Alan, faintly, when she had recovered
a little; having seen the danger he incurred.

"You have saved *me*," was the answer.

The commotion had now about spent itself;
some wounds and bruises had been inflicted
without any serious injuries. Ballatruim had
fared badly enough, as he deserved. He was
carried, sensible, though greatly bruised, to his
carriage. Alan conducted Miss Mar to her
party, who had waited for her at the door.

"I am of no political party," she said to
Alan, at parting. "Perhaps a lady should not
be; therefore I am able to appreciate truth and
great actions on whichever side I find them."
There was still a tone of condescension here,
of which the speaker herself was conscious!
Had her admiration not conquered that?

Alan spoke low a few words in answer.

"You may make the daughter of an old
Tory a decided believing Radical," she added,
more gaily.

"It is action, not cold belief, Miss Mar,

that is required. There are more believers—
passive believers—at heart than you know of,"
answered Alan, as they approached her party.
Her evident efforts to secure his esteem—bold
as these were, after what had occurred between
them at the Castle—mollified him while in her
presence, and there grew a softness in his ac-
cents towards her.

Throwing all the meaning permissible into
her response, she said, as she bade Alan good-
night, " I will not forget that there has been a
pleasant episode in to-night's adventure.   For
the rest I trust to time."   Alan turned to
greet Oliver Arnot, whose voice he heard behind him, but he had caught the full smile of
Miss Mar upon himself.   He knew its meaning, and he again lifted his hat as the party
drove off.

CHAPTER XIII.

ON the afternoon of an early day following the events narrated in the previous chapter, Alan was preparing to set out to continue an investigation into the cause of the riot at the church, when a messenger arrived from Morven Castle, with a letter addressed to him by Colonel Mar. The Colonel wished to see Alan, the first time he passed, anent the education of the female children of the parish.

The affair at the church had been the talk of the county on the Sunday and following days, and rumour, which had at the same time Colonel Mar's character in its care, had associated the commotion with some sinister design of the old Indian and his daughter. These rumours had already borne fruit, to the chagrin of Miss Mar, in the absence of the expected

civilities consequent upon her party and upon
her danger in the church, and in positive rudeness from some quarters.

"Where bound for, Alan?" asked old Macalpine, when he saw his son on horseback.
The old man had been jauntier since the lecture in the church. Fond of applause and
notoriety, that which his son received was
nourishment to him.

"To Morven Castle," was the answer.

"Gratifying their selfish pride," said the
father, placing emphasis on the last two words,
which he remembered were Alan's own in
speaking of Colonel Mar on a former occasion.
"But you are right—quite right; live by the
rising sun—not by the expiring candle; you
will be in the cold and the dark if you do
not." The laird's humour set adrift his marriage scheme.

Alan had had experience of taunts on the
part of his father. He knew that his father
was incapable of appreciating his character,

which was probably his deepest sorrow. Continual misconstruction by that one who in nature should know us truly, has a corroding influence, even upon the best of characters.

"Perhaps I am gratifying my own, rather," was his answer.

Roderick Macalpine was puzzled. As Alan went off, the laird shook his head. "There was something more than natural going on," which his philosophy could not find out.

It was Lucretia Mar whom Alan again saw alone on being admitted to the drawing-room of Morven Castle, and he at once thought that the communication he had received must have been inspired by her. She was again arrayed in that superb richness which a handsome person alone permits the wearer to adopt without being liable to a charge of ostentation. She did not permit her visitor on this occasion to walk alone the length of the long room,— meeting him nearly at the door, while she walked with him towards that window where

recently she had turned her eyes from him.
Now she looked out with him upon the river,
the oak-clad hill, and the blue mountain-peak
resting in calm majesty in the peace of a
summer night.

"I must apologise, Miss Mar, for not calling
personally on Sunday, rather than sending to
inquire for you," said Alan; "but you seemed
so little the worse, that I expected you would
be as it proved."

"I wished to see you," she said, with a look
of perfect frankness, "before you meet Colonel
Mar. I told you I belonged to no political
party: I have become a convert to yours.
Toryism is antiquated and tiresome."

"And what," asked Alan, somewhat amused,
"does Miss Mar expect by becoming a Radical,
as she doubtless names me. The first result
will be her father's displeasure, if not more."

"No," she replied; "I speak to you frankly:
my days have been spent among people whose
minds were covered with the cobwebs of age,

which they were too lazy to take the trouble
to remove. They regarded the world as they
saw it from their own door-steps, beyond which
they were not privileged to gaze. My father I
have only known within the last two years;
and he is silent, and broods upon the past,
which is his all in all. Society I have found
concerning itself only with the petty details
of its little life, its gaiety at the best assumed.
When Colonel Mar proposed purchasing this
estate in the Highlands, where I had never
been except in the romantic pages of Sir
Walter Scott, I was delighted beyond bounds,
and imagined such free existence everywhere
as you yourself pictured on Saturday. Judge,
then, my surprise and disappointment when I
find all the dreadful mediocrity of manner and
tameness of existence more fully displayed
than in London. The everlasting tittle-tattle
of the picture, or the new opera, were prefer-
able to a discussion of the movements of your
next door neighbour, or the height of his new

pony, or even the condition of the political roll of the county. Now I expect that, by becoming a Radical, I join a cause in which there is movement—colours to be won ; it will relieve me from the embarrassment of *ennui*, and the presence of fools."

Here was a situation,—a star of the first magnitude found in Alan the cynosure of her eyes. But Alan was wary.

"I sympathise with you, Miss Mar," he replied, " while I must say you are unacquainted with the world if you think to leap out of your situation in a moment. If you proclaim yourself to-morrow a Radical, I repeat, how will Colonel Mar regard the singularity ? "

"He will approve my exercise of my own judgment."

"And those about you, upon whom you are dependent for society ? "

"Let them receive it as they may. I am already sick of their commonplace airs, which, if they are those inherited of the Conqueror, or Fingal himself, very much dwarf the romance of history. No, sir; tell me at once how I may become a Radical."

"You are in the wrong quarter," said Macalpine, smiling, "applying to me for the declaration of party. I belong to none. I care little for party principles or cries. My ambition is to see the barriers destroyed which impede the progress of the people. I make no battle to acquire power for myself."

"You do not mean to say that you do not desire a seat in Parliament, with the rank and influence it brings. Permit me to say you would be likely to command more success there than the samples of members I have recently known."

"Perhaps so; but I have no such desire. Even if it were natural to entertain such a wish, I know that the happiness of myself and others would be best promoted by keeping out of it."

"Ah, you will change," said Miss Mar, as she swept round with the folds of her dazzling dress, while with a laugh of pleasing intimacy she looked into Macalpine's face. " I know you possess sufficient of the common and common-sense material of men to be able to come down from the height on which you now stand."

Lucretia Mar was evidently playing a game. She cared nothing for either political, phil-anthropic, patriotic, or any other principles whatever, even while she pretended to discuss them. She cared for power over something superior to the trifling objects upon which she found women everywhere prattling away their days. She had neither seen at her feet, nor yet heard of, the Highland lord of noble mien, chief of the mountains, master of the baronial halls, and disposer of lives of vassals.

But before her was one not incapable, by the advantages of nature and education, of realising her ideal hero. She saw in him more than the son of a ruined laird, though still deprived of all the vulgar yet necessary accessories to the idealization.

It was rather an incentive than a vexation to Lucretia Mar to find that, despite all this, she had a battle to fight ere the son of Roderick Macalpine would surrender to her charms. She saw plainly enough that his heart might have been in Kamtschatka for all the real influence over it she had yet exercised. His coldness but determined her upon double exertion. Here was work for her hitherto tame hours—to acquire the heart as well as the hand of the only man she had yet found worthy such exertion. It was not with any intention to be immolated that she decided upon winning him : her elevation to a throne of social eminence as the wife of a man of genius had large part in her passion. She imagined herself the centre of crowds distinguished in political and social life—in the ascendant against that array of tottering exclusiveness which she had uneasily looked upon, and was too proud to follow after. .

"Before you see Colonel Mar I have a boon

to ask of you," said Miss Mar, in her very
softest tones. "I have received a present
of this album, and my petition is that
you open it with a specimen of your own
powers."

Alan opened the album mechanically. At
the first page there he read what appeared to
give him pain. His face coloured; and with
his eyes riveted upon the lines before him,
he told Miss Mar that the book was already
provided with an opening inscription. She
answered she was not aware of it.

"Then you do not dissemble to surprise me,
Miss Mar," Alan said. "Here are transcribed
some doggerel lines, said to be of old date, and
to refer to my family. They were painful to
my mother—so much so as to cause her un-
comfortable nervous apprehensions when they
came into her head. I had buried their re-
collection. It is most strange to find them
here!"

"I never saw them before, and never heard

of the rhyme. How odd!" and she repeated
one of the verses :—

> " Macalpine's bluid will mix like wine,
> When Morven Castle he shall tyne ;
> Macalpine's heir will have his ain,
> Ere that lost bluid can run again."

" There is some mystery even in the hand-
writing," she continued. She added, thought-
fully, " Do you not take consolation from the
last two lines, which give back to the heir of
Macalpine the lands of Morven ? If there is
pain intended, it is for me, who am apparently
to be dispossessed—if the sting is not to be taken
out of the rhyme by keeping the word of promise
to sense and ear by some happy conformity."
This was said with so much good-humour that
Alan could not doubt her sincerity.

" Why do you not tear the doggerel out of
the book, Miss Mar ?" Alan inquired.

" I will burn the book itself if you desire it,
though it seems to me you have most reason
to keep the prophecy in remembrance," was
the answer.

"I see you do not believe in the prophecy," remarked Alan, with a seriousness which imposed upon his companion.

"Do you?" she inquired quickly, and with some eagerness.

"There are strange decrees in fate," he rejoined, dreamily; "and in the family of Macalpine there are records of what we term miraculous interpositions. They have been always falling, yet never have actually fallen; it has just been when they seemed incapable of ever again rising to the surface that they reach the haven."

Lucretia Mar's countenance fell and rose. "Then I have to contemplate all the horrors of ruin,—my father reduced to meanness, and I the schoolmistress of the parish, cleaning the dirty paws of peasant urchins, and torturing my imagination with the alphabet."

"If I were a believer in augury and your humility, I might consider such a picture justifiable by this mysterious presentation."

"I regard the intrusion of this rhyme as too serious an affair to treat lightly, and will be at the bottom of it," cried Miss Mar, scarcely knowing how to treat the seriously spoken banter of Alan. "Meantime, do me the favour to turn over the leaf and forget it. I cannot tear it out now. It may be true, and I not dispossessed," she continued, in gay familiarity.

"I am in no poet's mood, Miss Mar," remarked Alan. "I am unequal to the scribble."

"Then give me your last essay?" she asked.

"I amuse myself with the sonnet," Alan said, with a little flush; "but my last verses on a mountain daisy and a meadow rose might be displeasing to one I should compare rather with the latter than the humbler flower."

"Nay, nay," she answered, recovering still further to a sprightly humour. "I am all eagerness while you write; let me learn my character in allegory."

So Alan wrote; Miss Mar busying herself around, her fine form, in well-proportioned magnificence, seen in most graceful attitudes.

Two flowers there were gave incense to the morn.
　First in the mountain-pass a daisy grew,
Beside the tangled broom and homely thorn,
　That took my eyes from off all other hue ;
Methought it opened to my quest of view.
　Thus off more keenly cast the dew of night,
And spread its beauty to the breeze that blew,
　Pleasing itself and me with every might ;
Tricked in the sunbeam, it laughèd full out,
　And ducked as if the storm might come when will ;
No sucker of its sweets can put to rout
　The golden riches in its bosom still ;
Ne'er truer flower upon the mountain grows
Than that sweet blossom which my summer knows.

In splendour decked, a rose in meadow lay.
　Not all the foliage of the land might vie
The colour rich, the leaves that scent the day,
　The pride that spoke to every floweret by ;
Beneath the sun how boldly stood the bloom,
　And to its luscious life each passer fain—
Its fondest wish was to evade the gloom,
　Full knowing well how ill it stood the pain
Of severance from its well nurtured store,
　Which base intruders might all wreck with greed,
Or falling cloud disperse as thing of yore,
　And it despair because of very need ;
In this the pamper of a better born—
The hardy way-flower of its virtue shorn.

After he had written the verses, he handed the album to his companion, who read them aloud. She shut and laid down the book, and turned away with an affectation of indigna· tion. "You were shocked," she said, returning to Alan, and smiling through seeming vexation, "to find written this mysterious prophecy of my weak inheritance, and yet you follow it up with a comparison unfavourable to my strength of character. Is not this cruel ?"

"I could have no right to depict Miss Mar's character upon so short an acquaintance. The *second* sonnet is drawn from imagination alone," observed Alan, without raising his eyes, but with marked emphasis.

She did not inquire whether the first sonnet had been inspired by experience. She looked as if she wished not to know further.

"I observe," she said, "that you set yourself to extol simplicity."

"Simple truth, miscalled simplicity," repeated Alan, interrupting her, " in the words of the world's truest poet. It is simple truth to extol the sweetness and refinements of nature which are within the reach of all, above the coarse and costly exaggerations of the conventional world."

She gave a shrug of good-humoured incredulity.

" Ah ! " replied Alan, " ' true happiness costs little ; if it be dear it is not of good quality,' says Chateaubriand. That is my own experience. You still ask if all this be sincere—if it be not merely the humour of the hour, to give the preference to the natural over that material glitter with which society has invested all its belongings. The love of nature is written indelibly in my heart ; when it fades life itself will be feeble, and I will know decay and death have placed their first mark upon me."

Macalpine paused. Miss Mar was gratified that he so spoke. No woman of ability but will love a man of talent for addressing himself to her intellect. "Go on," she observed, her expression evidencing complete interest.

He hesitated; but he thought he read a sincerity. His stern enthusiasm had had its influence. "The world's truest spirits," he continued, "have always sickened on its pomp, though woman probably wearies only at the last." There was a deep romantic melancholy in the shade which passed over the speaker's face. It did not fail to entrance his companion. She felt for an instant a reality present to her greater than the realities she had only hitherto believed in. She had seen the reflection of far off passion, of a heart which had stirred in these solitary wilds at many a sadness, and moved with many an aspiring glow, capable of the deepest love.

"Since the world began, men have been as fond as women of the pomp of life," urged Miss Mar, as Alan's slowly spoken sentence ceased. "You are not quit with its richer gaieties; do not tell me so."

" Why ? " he asked.

"You are a poet, are you not? The mere
march and array—' the pomp, pride, and circumstance '—have as much claim on poetic
imaginations as the cause of battle."

" Not in my case; my aspirations are too
serious. I am ever painfully alive to the end
of things; and if I permit myself to indulge in
illusions, I hope it is never when a worthy
cause is in progress. Besides, I do not follow
after the poetry of our day. Do you know
why I prefer Homer and Shakespeare? Not
for the gorgeousness of their diction: for the
simplicity of their thoughts. What modern
rhymer has strength and light enough to make
his hero sigh for the sight of the smoke of his
own chimney, or seek the hatchet and the plough
while he is retained in the sublime? You remember Ulysses yearned to escape from the
arms even of a goddess, that he might retire to
his wife and child, and watch the smoke of his
own Ithaca. He was a wood-cutter, and the

maker of his bed, and challenges the skill of
the suitor to sow a meadow and drive the
straight furrow down the field. These simple
habits and loves are not now sung, the practice of them being obloquy, if not contempt.
The man who casts off showy ambition and
success, and works in the fields, is either eccen-
tric or incapacitated."

Lucretia Mar was puzzled; the whole matter
was new to her as a new world. While certainly not convinced, the fervid manner of
Macalpine held possession of her mind for the
time. Utopian she believed his aspirations
to be. As with many eternal truths to which
the world listens and is supposed to believe in,
the voice was just so much sound. Yet she,
strangely, accepted his expression of his mind
as simply a feeler on his side, ere he sought
what must delight him to win.

After a pause, in which she appeared to re-
flect, and Alan inclined as if to leave her, she
said, brightly,—" You cannot leave me only

half your way of thinking, as a sportsman
leaves the wounded bird, finding it not worth
more shot, or the trouble of carriage. Colonel
Mar will be waiting for you ; but tell me
when we may resume discussion—at present I
am *hors de combat.*"

The haughty woman bent down with a
little feeling of submission which could not be
assumed; so naturally plaintive, if insinuating,
became the grace of her speech, catching the
full animate eyes of the man she addressed, as
his heart swelled upon thoughts of the past, and
which the sweet spirit of Ellen Lee had not
aroused with violence, as apparently the contact
with this dark strong woman had done. Alan
expressed himself as honoured by the pupilage
of the lady. Soon thereafter he was gone from
her presence.

Upon Macalpine leaving the room, Miss Mar
sat gazing upon the pages of the album, now
thinking of the lines before her as somehow
bearing upon her own destiny, then abstracted

upon him who had left her. She had been affected in that interview as she had never been with man, observing well the traces of the influence which any woman of no common material can exert, when she tries, over the feelings of a man not unimpressionable to the charms of her sex. What though he were difficult? She believed in the omnipotence of her gold. Most women would have shrunk at a purchase: not so Lucretia Mar. She had a masculine temper, and as a man buys a pretty woman, so she felt she could call a lord of the creation to her side, by her talisman.

Nearly an hour passed away, and Miss Mar still sat before her album, when Colonel Mar entered the room. He was as tame looking as his daughter was animated—in the old worn dressing-gown which wrapped his shrivelled frame, and with his demure face, he appeared more like a draggled sparrow than a soldier.

"Lucretia, I have changed my mind," he mumbled.

She looked surprised, and rose hastily, bit-
ing her lip.

" My intention is to shoot the father ; not to
ask you to marry the son."

She was lately more surprisingly accustomed
to his strange humours.   She decidedly thought
that recent excitement had affected his brain.

" It is too late," she cried, however ;. "he
knows I love him."

Colonel Mar growled, with a fierce sternness
which she understood, " You must forget
him."

She buried her face in her stern pride from
the light of the day.   Had Alan Macalpine
known her then, a deep sympathy would at
once have rested in his heart for this woman.

"Ah, Lucretia," the Colonel said, seeing the
open album, " you have already read this old
woman's rhyme.   It has been cast in my teeth
more than once since our coming, and I have
begun to dream nightly of it.   I have had a
horrid feeling in connection with it, and I have

adopted the prescription of having it written down, that I may dispel the goblin of imagination with familiarity." He spoke with a humour ill at ease. He was haunted by other pain than the goblin rhyme.

"But no more, Lucretia, about this," he said, resuming his old quiet indifferent manner; "we shall be the laughing-stock of the county. You have, as usual, been too precipitate. You may make a grand selection with your fortune. This Highland vanity irritates me to distraction."

Colonel Mar shuffled away as he had entered. His daughter remained, sitting alone, until the few stars of the summer night were visible through the darkness of the room.

Macalpine learned from Colonel Mar that he was desirous to establish a school for girls, and he asked the assistance of Alan in carrying out the design. The proprietor of Morven had reflected long upon the interview which Alan had had with him, resulting largely in in-

creased admiration of the character of the son
of his predecessor ; and the report which his
daughter brought to him of the lecture and
conduct of Alan in the church, had determined him to seek the aid of so active a spirit
in a scheme of doing good. He believed Alan
to be reasonable, and he thought they would
get on so well together that he might almost
urge certain things for young Macalpine's own
benefit.   It happened that, although they
agreed altogether about the school, in the
promotion of which Alan eagerly offered his
best services, that when Colonel Mar came to
make a suggestion as to Alan's own affairs,
he again ruffled the delicate pride of the
young Highlander, who drew back with a
pain and chagrin he did not altogether conceal. They parted as friends, but a breach
had been made, not to be healed in a day, so
far as the Colonel was concerned, piqued, as
he had been so often, at what he deemed the
world's ingratitude.

The meeting in the church, followed by the
interview with Lucretia Mar, startled Alan.
What was only at first a fanciful apprehension,
suddenly dispelled, had turned mysteriously,
as it seemed to him, into a reality. Not possessing a particle of vanity, he was at loss to
account for her advances. He knew the nature
of this woman too well, nurtured, too, as she
was, in the school of mammon, to believe that
personal attractions, however high, would outweigh the sense of his poverty and his fallen
state. Yet what fortune could he have possibly awaiting him? He had been little in
the society of a woman like this—superb in
person, in adornment, in force and ease of
bearing, such as a knowledge of power gives
its possessor, most of all in the case of the
strong ones of the fair creation. Marred as
her character was, in his exacting estimate of
the sweetness and light which a true woman
should possess, he was not insensible to a certain charm, to which his poetic mobility, had

it not been under the guidance of a strong will, might have made him a victim. Before his eyes, for many minutes following his exit from the Castle, arose that splendid form ; in his ears spoke the rich commanding voice ; around him lay the noble old lands ; and the venerable Castle was at his back ; and he reeled more than once, with a wild sensation that all these might be his. But he was still able to penetrate beneath the dazzling surface.

He took his way to Finzean House ; and ere he was within its walls, his serene and loftier mind settled. He had gone purposely off his proposed course to think and talk of her in whose absence he had idealised something more than was perhaps well. The poet may for a time be better content with inditing sonnets to his mistress's eyebrows than in seeing her bustling among his household gods ; but his mistress has no gain in his satisfaction. Alan had wished to consider the mutual silence as an acknowledged penance for their too eager

devotion to each other; and he filled his
unoccupied hours dreaming, often with pen
in hand, of the fair Ellen of Finzean. This
must now end : he must at once, and, by every
effort in his power, bring to a conclusion
that
> "Suit,
> Full of poise and difficulty,
> And fearful to be granted,"

which a brave man's imagination will call upon
him to undertake. That Ellen was yet con-
stant to him he never doubted. He was the
son of a ruined proprietor, and had, according
to usage, to work his way in the world; and
he thought Ellen had fled from him in a belief
that she stood in the way of his progress.
Whispers had reached his ears that her people
thought he had been too lavish and free in his
conduct. There were not wanting those who,
still looking upon a Macalpine as a mighty
man in the land, said it was not for an "un-
kent lass," be she Oliver Arnot's niece as was
said, to keep company with young Macalpine;

and that it would turn out ill for both. Alan was indignant, as he might be; and he was angry with Ellen, when he heard these whispers, for making her sudden disappearance, which he could not but partly connect with them. Alan believed that he would have difficulty in persuading Ellen Lee to become his wife, were he successful in discovering her. There may be a hundred poor difficulties, or none at all, in the way of commonplace lovers; with the subtile, romantic spirit there may be one difficulty which is noble in the creation, and which no mere persuasion will ever remove.

As he waited for the farmer in his upper room his anxiety increased, the more that he had now an opportunity of making a substantial offer to Ellen. He had been asked by Colonel Mar to look out for a superintendent for the new school; and with delight he already saw her working independently a while beside himself in this fine field of usefulness.

CHAPTER XIV

WHAT were Ellen Lee's feelings as she was free of Finzean, and found herself settled for the time in a humble lodging in Edinburgh?

Before her was the vista of a commonplace street, and beyond the prospect of some scantily remunerated labour. But as the well-doing are almost never without some worthy being honestly attached to their welfare, and capable of that warmth of confidence which woman especially craves for, so she was not alone in the large city while she possessed the friendship of the mistress of the humble house where she lodged. Mrs Martha Macbean had periodically visited Ellen's mother ever since Ellen could remember, and they were on the most familiar terms. She was an old acquaintance, though of humbler stock than the Arnots, and had occasionally rendered Mrs Lee assistance in times of unusual occupation or distress. Ellen was the most beloved of the good woman's heart; and when she left Finzean she thought at once of a residence with Mrs Macbean, till she might procure some situation to maintain herself. Martha received her in gladness of spirit, with which she could not have welcomed any other living creature.

There is always a certain amount of pain in any change; but that which, looked fully at, beckons a great sorrow, is by the wise kept much away by other observation. So Ellen was even consoled in observing the new world that passed her by.

After much deferred hope, she procured a situation as governess in the family of a wealthy shopkeeper. The wages were barely sufficient for her maintenance, but she was glad of the employment, having already begun to feel the dulling influence of idleness; and her necessities being moderate, while her wardrobe was ample, she considered she would be able to "make both ends meet." She preferred teaching to the work of the sempstress, as she would herself receive an impetus to mental improvement, though she was on the point of engaging herself in the latter capacity, and, even with all her dignity and elevation of character, was prepared to accept humbler employment—which society, silly in its estimates, would judge as placing her beneath a ban. For this spirit she was indebted to Alan Macalpine, who had often expressed his sympathy with the condition of Ellen's sex, doomed to contumely simply because they preferred to eat the bread of industry rather than idleness.

It was late in the spring ere Ellen procured employment, and the summer passed quickly in activity at her work. She was fond of children, though, being an only child, she had little experience of their humours, which she now found full of interest and amusement.

The house was exceedingly dull without the

children ; and Ellen believed herself, with all her sense of loneliness, poverty, and present defeat, the happiest person in it. Her employer was a civic dignitary ; and between the eagerness of his talent for business and for municipal honours, he made a sad mess. He was all self—a terrible sample of that kind of it which grows from without, and not from within. In his presence Ellen had felt, with all his heartiness, as if the ideal in her nature suffered a sense of depression, even of struggling for bare life. His wife was a soft woman, with a large flabby heart,—the concomitant of a husband feared and admired,—tender, without fibre. They lived together no real life. At home, at social gatherings, at church, they were ever the same—without a conviction, without a purpose ; leading the hand-to-mouth life of ready-money people, proud of the fact, and incapable of appreciating any truth beyond it. John Jenkins was a loud and embellished parrot ; Mrs Jenkins was the machine upon

which the effect of his screeches was visible.
Their children were rude and noisy, but natural, and even kind, and amenable to instruction. Ellen took a deep interest in the work
of training them in a healthy conduct of themselves—the more that she saw the incapacity
of their parents for instructing them.

In the beginning of August, Ellen had a
week's holiday ; and Mrs Macbean, wishing
also a few days in the country, desired Ellen
to say where they might spend the time together, hinting her own preference for the
district, not very far off, where she visited in
the days of Mrs Lee. So Ellen and she went
there.

Ellen visited former friends ; but her altered
fortune, which she was in her true courage at
no pains to conceal, cooled their interest, even
where they did not turn their backs upon her.
Ellen had been partly alive to the expectation of
this, but her worthy companion felt the affront
bitterly. She did not hide her resentment,

muttering about "gentle blood" being better than "thae bodies wi' a kail-yard an' a yard-stick"—a combination of small-proprietorship and shopocracy which Mrs Macbean evidently considered most contemptible. In unmistake-able language Ellen learned scandal concerning her dead mother; yet she left without bitter-ness.

On the evening of the day preceding their intended leave of the little town, the coach from the west overtook them as they entered the town. Public conveyances were then more than now objects of great interest to every one. All looked with eager eyes, in and out, as the coach passed along, or drew up at the hostelry, in vague longing after some friend who might be travelling.

Mrs Macbean and Ellen stopped, as the coach drew up at some little distance from them; and with mingled feelings, beside sur-prise of the moment, did Ellen find herself discovered by Alan Macalpine.

Ellen had made Mrs Macbean no confidant of the short passage in her life which concerned Alan, because she desired to forget it as she could; while that worthy lady would fain have kept it alive, being rather a glutton of tales of love and romance. It was better now to break the matter to her at once.

"Martha," Ellen said, "I have only kept one secret from you, because I wished it to be one even from myself. I know it would die with you if necessary; for who trusted you like my mother? I am to tell you it now: I have been in love."

"Is that your secret, lassie!" said Mrs Macbean, laughing; "I could know that without the telling,—though, as you have not spoken o't, I have never asked you who is the pretty gentleman."

"He is leaving the coach yonder now," said Ellen, tremulously.

"And comes to carry you away a bonnie bride?"

"My fears have not carried me that length. I thought to have forgot our acquaintance; but he may now have come to find me out, and bring me to book for leaving Finzean."

"And you have run from him? and your working and seeking my house comes of this? Well, well, Ellen, I suspected like it, though I thought little and said nothing at all. God be praised for your sense and happy temper, and give you the man of your heart, laird or lord; it's no siller ye've sought, though may be it's the man that can point to his fathers before him; for it's Macalpine's son I warrant me that's ta'en your fancy."

"How could you know that, Martha?" inquired Ellen, who observed the old lady to pause suddenly. "Some one has told you."

"That they hae," cried Mistress Martha; 'you're simple, my love, to think I didna ken. You forget I was born near his lands. Ah, I remember the auld laird well in his hey-day, as fine a fellow as ever walked the heather;

and his wife, too, as gentle and considerate a lady as the best, for all the story of her elopement. If his son be like him, gude be here, but you'll be married the morn!"

Ellen assured her companion she need have no fear of that.

"In love and not marry!" cried the advocate against single blessedness; "what's life without that? I'm thinking many a cauld man and many a saucy lass have repented their ways before the snows of age befell them. You'll maybe both of you be needing gear—that may be. But when Colin and I married, we had just two hundred pounds to sit down with—enough; enough and more it was, for we found both ends meet and had pleasure at the job, and at laying by for the rainy day that came ower soon, for the Lord ended our wedded happiness in this world in the heat of our best summer. The siller always comes to the stout heart, be the brae stey as it likes."

"Reflection has told me," said Ellen, after a pause, as they approached the door of their lodging, "that marriage between those of unequal rank is not likely to conduce to the happiness of either."

"And who says that Macalpine and you are of unequal rank?" inquired Mrs Macbean, excitedly.

Ellen would have had her curiosity excited by the peremptory manner of her companion, had all her thoughts not been occupied with the prospect of the forthcoming encounter. But the circumstance did not altogether escape her, and her mind recurred to it afterwards.

"The daughter of a village surgeon does not match with the chief of a Highland clan, though the latter may be the last to proclaim it," was all she said.

Mrs Macbean hurried to her own room in a state of extreme excitement. Ellen sat down at the back of their parlour. She was no coward, to fly from him who sought now to

confront her, yet she had to screw her courage
to the sticking place. She knew that her
firmness would be put to the test. When she
heard Alan's clear and deliberate voice in the
passage, she had an impulse to run out and
welcome him as she had so often done at
Finzean. But she controlled herself.

They shook hands, and Alan sat down scarcely
invited; Ellen having lost speech altogether
for a minute.

He could not pronounce his opinion of the
situation in one single word, and he was
anxious not to upbraid her. He came in as
he would have done at Finzean, and his frank
spirit felt chilled by the reception he met with.

"Ellen, why did you run away? you have
given me a strange time of it, and a hard race,"
he observed, quietly. She could not answer
so direct a question satisfactorily. "Had I
offended you or done you wrong?" he inquired, with more warmth.

"No!" she answered with spirit, remember-

ing the character and principles of the man
beside her. "I fled because I could not deliberate. I had done wrong; my happiness
at Finzean was entirely selfish, and in the end
must have proved delusive."

The revelation restored Alan. He experienced a glow of pride in the increased charm
of Ellen's voice.

There was less passivity and not less tenderness in her countenance; deeper reflection and
more experience of the world had heightened
its expression. Her emotions were more real,
and her sense and appreciation of life fuller.

He wished to save her further trial, while
the roots of his love, as he sat there, went
deeper by his sympathy, and his pain, which
was mixing with joy.

"But why not remain at Finzean? Happiness is too often rudely shocked by a blow
from others, that we should ourselves fly from
it when we possess it," Alan said.

"I could no longer, too, be a burden on my

uncle," she repeated, wishing to make no other explanation on that head.

"Ellen, you feared I should pay the bond I owed you; why do you fly then from me? Return with me."

"I cannot," she cried, interrupting him.

"Let us understand each other," he said, alarmed that he had been misunderstood, or her heart somehow poisoned against him. "You did not think it possible that I was— that we passed the idle hours for our amusement only; you cannot believe this, you know better; you needed no formal proffer of my love."

"I am not fitted for you," answered Ellen, constrained to speak. "You owe a duty to your blood, your kin,—to your birth, and to your history,—to your misfortunes, which I cannot share. Had I rank and wealth to offer, then it might be so; but as it is, you would cripple, ruin your highest interests, and perhaps also mine."

"Oh Ellen!"——

"Your people," she continued, regardless of the interruption, "regard you as the head of the house—that one alone who can restore the family inheritance, or at least lay the foundation-stone of the building to be completed in two or more generations. If you cast this obligation aside, to wed the penniless child of a country doctor, you forfeit their affection—nay, their very look, their name, and kinship—for ever; while I am the fated object of their hate, and must look to be the creature for your father's gibes and curses, if not harder ill-will. You consider solely your own feelings: consider your obligations to your position in your particular world, and to your family—to me. I will learn to forget an error of my simpler days, as I call upon you also to do so."

"I appreciate your noble motive, Ellen," answered Alan; "but it is founded on illusions rather than realities. It is in vain to remind me of conventional obligations; my father alone I have to consider. That has been done. As for the rest, it is silence—-my mother would have approved. I have no ambition whatever to be restored to Morven. Think you I would be so free and happy with it? And I do not intend to immolate myself beneath the car of any deity of this world."

" I am convinced," answered Ellen, " of the justice of your heart ; but I have bowed to other authority, as we all do who would live rightly. I believe you will have to bow to it." She repeated the last sentence with as strong an emphasis as she could muster. "Your father believes in your restoration to the estates of Morven : ally yourself with me, and he finds in my person that which renders it impossible."

Lucretia Mar came before Alan's mind. Was it possible that Ellen had heard and believed the rumours concerning them? It was evident she knew something. Pettishness in such circumstances would have been, with

smaller natures, the cause of much that Ellen
was saying; with hers Alan was convinced it
was not.   Alan was determined to be out with it.

"Some absurd gossip has surely armed you
with this suggestion.   Why an alliance with
you should render the realisation of my father's
dream impossible, I know not.   It is true that
the new proprietor's presumptive heir is a
daughter, and unmarried, which latter I also
am; but beyond these two facts there is no
circumstance to work out the vision.   Gossips
may do so who weave their idle webs."

It almost seemed as if Ellen smiled.   "I
have heard from my uncle simply that you
were on terms of intimacy with Colonel Mar
and his daughter," she said.

"It was by accident—very far from my
choice—that the intimacy arose," broke in
Alan.   His directness told against him; while
it really had soothed Ellen's spirits, it now
gave her the cue to a defiant reconciliation
with her course.

"You do not believe," Ellen continued, "that I have been otherwise than interested in all that concerns Morven, where it would be false to say I did not pass the happiest months of my life ; and I will continue to feel interested still. Of the fortunes of all in it will I care' to hear, and of none more than of yours."

She had spoken with a deliberate but painful firmness which was costing her much ; her last expression was the formalism of the mind, hurriedly predominant, where the heart is weeping and seeking for escape. She rose. But it was with a dignity in which her tenderness was gone in the victory of a high spirit, which she had summoned to aid her in this moment of trial, when she feared she might prove no match for the persuasive powers of the man whose love, under other circumstances, she might have filled her existence with.

There remained really nothing more for

Alan to say. He respected the temper of the
mistress of his heart too much, and was himself too proud and sensitive, to hammer out
the argument of his suit further. He had yet
to tell, however, the immediately practical
design of his coming ; and he spoke low and
distantly, but kindly. "You will allow me to
ask, Ellen, if you are happy where you are ?"
he inquired.

"Quite," she answered.

"I knew you preferred the country to the
town," he went on, "and a new situation as
teacher at Morven having opened up, I had
thought you might have accepted it."

"Thanks, many thanks, for thinking of me,
but at present I could not think of changing
my employment."

Alan turned from her, seeing that a pro-
longation of the interview was painful. They
shook hands together at parting, without a
word of "good-bye" or "*au revoir*."

"I will try to forget this meeting," said Alan.

"You must forget me too; it is what I demand," said Ellen Lee.

"Never!" cried Alan.

And he was alone in the dull street of the little town.

Alan would fain have taken all for that serious play of lovers which is only a drama where all ends well. But he was without any real hope. He knew that Ellen appreciated his character as too serious, earnest, and proud to descend to entreaty ; and how could he ever approach her again with the language of his suit? Never!

Ellen looked into the room where her old friend was as patient as she could be,—the spirit which she had summoned not having yet gone down. The sight of the faithful and only companion of her loneliness brought her back to tenderness. She could not help showing what she had done.

"How have you done this, Ellen?" said her companion, gently.

" He may wed another who may restore his estate."

" You *have* loved him ?"

" With my whole heart," cried the meek spirit, feeling content to have been loved and to have renounced for his sake.

" May God in heaven reward you !" Mrs Macbean wept tears of sorrow and of regret. Ellen went away. It was an hour and more before her companion joined her in their little parlour.

END OF VOL. 1.

PRINTED BY BALLANTYNE AND COMPANY
EDINBURGH AND LONDON

www.ingramcontent.com/pod-product-compliance
Lightning Source LLC
Chambersburg PA
CBHW031344020726
47499CB00005B/1390